Thorns of Life

David G Maillu

Moran (E. A.) Publishers Limited,
Judda Complex, Prof. Wangari Maathai Road,
P. O. Box 30797, Nairobi.

With offices and representatives in: Uganda, Rwanda, Tanzania, Malawi and
Zambia

www.moranpublishers.com

First published 1988, Macmillan Publishers Limited

This edition, Moran (EA) Publishers Limited, 2017

ISBN 978 9966 63 023 0

2020		2019		2018		2017	
8	7	6	5	4	3	2	1

Prelude

This is a family story of a mother, son, and daughter-in-law, namely Kalunde, Maweu and Nzivele respectively. It is told within the background of the modern stormy cultural transition that is sweeping through Africa creating social havocs. Fate has thrown Kalunde's impoverished life to depending on her married son, whereby the burdened daughter-in-law is the one to call shots while, she is struggling to bear the mean marriage lived in the hostile and fast-changing countryside life. In spite of Kalunde's life plagued by a trail of desolation, she tries her best to hold together the thin threads of her son's shaky marriage but at a very high price.

Maillu, who wears many hats of talents, established himself as the most widely read and controversial writer in East Africa in 1970s where he won a unique position. He is famed for frankness, humour and deep insight into his society, with wide range of creative publications that include essays. He has also written and published extensively for children in English, Kiswahili and Kikamba. He holds a PhD in African Literature and Political Philosophy.

1

$\blacklozenge \ \blacklozenge \ \blacklozenge \ \blacklozenge$

It was uncomfortable, unpleasant, fearful and painful to her. She returned to the house with clenched teeth, fighting against tears. She withdrew into herself on the double bed, curled up like a wounded spider and burst into tears to relieve all that shaking.

However, nobody had shaken her; nobody had even touched or harassed her. Instead, she had just killed an animal – a dog they called Makenzi. It was the way Makenzi had died that had wounded Swastika Nzivele. She hadn't liked watching the dog in its dying throes, although she had been unable to help herself.

It was on a Friday, around eleven o'clock in the morning. Swastika Nzivele had given Makenzi a piece of poisoned meat two hours earlier. At first, Makenzi seemed to withstand the poison very well. He barked proudly as usual to passing people in order to impress his mistress, who had given him that rare, big piece of meat. Nzivele had wanted to go to Koola Town that day but she had cancelled her appointment. She would go only after finding out whether the poison that the Indian in Masaku had given her was real or some fake substance. Would it be effective on Makenzi who looked too strong to be broken by any force of death?

Makenzi played with the chickens joyfully, running after them; and with the twin goat kids which were two months old. By then, Nzivele was lying on her bed listening to some cool, sentimental music on her stereo. She lay on her back, her hands over her breast, her legs folded but twitching spasmodically, opening and closing her thighs like the wings of a butterfly. This particular album had made her shed tears many a time. She would weep and weep listening to it yet would not stop, repeating it again and again as if she enjoyed the crying. This time, she rolled her head gently with the rhythm, her hands still over her breast, her eyes staring blankly at the ceiling, like a newly orphaned child reliving her past.

When she came out later to check on Makenzi, she found him basking in the sun, lying straight on his stomach, not on his side, his chin stretched out on the ground, his eyes half-shut. Certainly, Nzivele noticed, there was some change in him; his hair was a little bit ruffled as if he was cold. Nzivele hung herself by her hands at the door and watched Makenzi.

Although Makenzi heard her movements, he didn't look at her. He remained motionless, breathing heavily, rather inconsistently. He coughed and sent a cloud of dust from his nose, still keeping his muzzle on the ground. He hiccupped. She watched with fearful interest, chewing her nails, some of the disturbance she felt showing on her puckered face. She was all alone in her home.

When Makenzi began to die a short time later, the incident was rough and dramatic. He went round and round the house, head bent, walking with a lop sided gait, trotting or going slowly, puffing big coughs that stretched and squeezed his stomach like bellows. Then he began to move in circles, sweeping glances across the sky, twice coming to Nzivele imploringly to feel her touch. But she drove him away, twisting her face.

'*Thi!*' she cursed.

He went and lay down but got up as soon as his body had touched the ground. His ruffled hair made him look darker and wild. Now he began to howl continuously, squeaking and twisting his body. Nzivele became frightened. She felt something tug at her heart and wished she could do something to save Makenzi from the pain.

'Oh no!' she cried and blocked her mouth with her hand. 'Oh my God, what can I give him!' She moved a little, back into the house, and watched, her heart beating fast.

Too far gone for any aid, Makenzi died rolling on the ground, growling and digging himself into the soil, his head beating helplessly for life while Nzivele watched, horrified. She was convinced that when Makenzi finally breathed his last, his eyes, which seemed full of tears, were on her. The dog excreted, shook violently two or three times, then died.

It was that very ending of Makenzi's life, the helplessness in his eyes and the struggle, that hit Nzivele so hard. In that moment she hated herself, realising how ungrateful and unkind she had been to a dog who had always dedicated his life to serve her to his maximum ability. She cried bitterly, squeezing her head between her hands.

But all that was a mere passing dark cloud. She didn't cry for long. She recovered very fast, gathered her spirits together, sheathed her beautiful legs in a pair of red trousers and went to call a neighbour a mile away to come to help her to bury Makenzi, if not to be at least a witness to Makenzi's death.

The technicalities of Makenzi's death were not the issue however. The real issue was that, from now onwards, Makenzi could bark no more in the night, particularly when Simon Mosi was coming to pay Swastika Nzivele a visit. She lived house-to-house with her mother-in-law, Kalunde Muthungu. Nzivele's husband, Silvesta Maweu, worked in Mombasa as an accountant in a bank. There were two hundred and forty miles between the couple, between Maweu and Nzivele at her country home in Kyandumbi.

2

◆ ◆ ◆ ◆

To talk more about Swastika Nzivele, her husband Silvesta Maweu and Simon Mosi is, altogether, to steal the story from the rightful owner, Kalunde Muthungu. Indeed, had it not been for Kalunde, Nzivele would either have been living with her husband in Mombasa or working somewhere. How often did Nzivele wonder whether it was by design that one has no control over one's life and things must be what they are? This should really have been Kalunde's question.

These last years of Kalunde's life were stiff ones, mainly because she was an old woman, now in her eighties. In those past years, in the years of her youth and energy, she had been a strong, capable woman. She must have transported many tons of load on her back during her active life, and she must have cultivated, altogether, hundreds of square miles of ground. But no one dodges old age, or death either. The weight of age had withered the strong Kalunde down into a weak person, with very poor eyesight.

All that, added to the condition in which she lived at that time, wrote a big question mark in her mind over what life was all about. But she bore it, practically and with minimum bitterness, knowing well that life is your own burden; only when you are dead, she thought, does your body become other people's burden to bury.

Kalunde would have been in a better position if the river near her home hadn't existed in that particular place. She had lost four of her family to the torrents of the River Kaiti, beginning with her husband, Muthungu, worse still, he tried to save their three children from being carried away by its raging waters.

This had happened one morning, just before noon. Kalunde's two sons and a daughter had gone down to the river to fetch some water in their gourds. Muthungu was working in his garden by the family home, preparing it for planting. The rains had not yet started. But any time, from the look of the clouds, it was going to pour.

In the late hours of the previous night, there had been a huge rainstorm around Kiimakiu, far from Kyandumbi, at the source of the River Kaiti, which had then passed westwards into Maasailand. But in Kyandumbi the morning arrived brightly, all sunshine as usual. Nobody would have thought it had rained anywhere. By eleven in the morning, the ground was roasting with heat; too hot already for those who walked barefoot, so they now avoided the bare path and walked on the grass. Today it was still, humid, and unpleasant. Those who sweated did so profusely. Kalunde had drunk water the previous day, a sign that it was going to rain within one or two days to come. Only when the rains were that close did her body ask for water.

Kalunde's children were deep in the well dug in the sand on the riverbed when the villagers up the river, who first saw the water sweeping down, started screaming, sounding a warning that there was a flash-flood running down the river bed. Since the previous night's rainstorm, the flood had been coming down through the hilly country. As the Kaiti has a sloping river bed, the water usually comes down swiftly, beating the banks and rocks and splashing many up with resounding explosions.

Muthungu heard the scream rather late and remembered his children. He flew down the slope instantly, yelling at the top of his voice as if he expected his words to stop the water from flowing. The children didn't hear his call, or those of the villagers, or maybe they heard them too late. Muthungu's were not the only children down there. There were ten of them, and they were playing noisily, chasing each other and wrestling on the sand. None of them escaped.

Muthungu was overpowered at the last minute trying to save his daughter who had made an attempt to escape. A mighty wave hit the wall of the bank they were just about to climb. The wall collapsed, claiming extra ground above it where Muthungu and his daughter were. Both fell into the stormy waters and disappeared. It was as if an enormous dam had broken upriver. At the time Kalunde had been heavily pregnant with Silvesta Maweu.

Kalunde never had another child after Maweu, for she did not remarry. Maweu grew up as her only hope of security for her old age. She had to wait for a long time before he became a man; she did so trusting that when he grew up, he would take on the farm they had by River Kaiti. If good work was done on this farm, she would have a soft old age.

But somehow, things didn't follow the course of her dreams. If they followed that course at all, they never did quite meet Kalunde's main expectations. The years that saw Maweu through his secondary education were very tough years for Kalunde's home was plagued by one famine after another. In times of tears and when the famine wasn't on the rampage, she kept faith with her dreams, for she had to live for her son. She tried her best to see that he had education. How often had she walked all the way from Kyandumbi to Nunguni and back? It must have been a twenty miles return journey, up and down the sloping and stony sides of Kilungu Hill, carrying a kyondo full of commodities she had brought to trade at Koola Market. She would have a load of sugar-cane, or bananas, or sweet potatoes, or cassava . . . which she would sell and on which she would make, in some cases, a profit of ten shillings when the times were good, though less, much less, during bad times. She could carry out this trade four times a month, for the market day was only once every week.

She always worried Maweu by the size of load she could carry on her back, which seemed to be three times her body size. As she walked, you saw the weight of the load in the knots of her calf muscles which supported her and in the way her toes gripped the ground, her feet grinding hard particles of soil as she walked. She had never worn shoes during her entire life, for those were the times women wore no shoes and only a few men were beginning to wear tyre sandals.

As Kalunde didn't have any other help in her home, her garden went unprepared most of the time. Each farming season found the garden more of a jungle. She either didn't have money to hire oxen for ploughing or by the time she got the money, it was too late for planting. She could only manage to cultivate a small patch of the garden that hardly yielded enough for food. Had it not been for some bananas that Muthungu had planted before he died, her wishes for Maweu's education would not have been realised.

You felt Kalunde's hardship when you shook hands with her. Her hands were rough, like the body of a lizard, black and with cracks, spoilt by the milk of the green bananas that had to be peeled every day for cooking. Her lips were rough too, and her teeth discoloured because of handling the green bananas. But her pretty heels, even as she grew old, never bore a single crack. If you ignored the roughness of her skin, the slightly unpleasant smell that she left behind after passing you and looked into her eyes properly, searching for the person who lived in that body, you would see a woman you could admire. Where there are no flowers in a garden it takes an artist's mind to see beauty there.

When the famine struck especially hard, the Kyandumbi night thieves seemed to gang together to steal nearly every edible green banana in Kalunde's garden. Then she had to suffer. The thieves seemed bent on destroying the garden rather than just taking what they wanted; they stripped the pumpkin vines off their leaves, which they took to cook, uprooted the old and young cassava plants in search of any edible roots, and so on. Nobody was happy with the situation for nobody liked stealing . . . it was due to the desperation of hungry men. The villagers understood everything.

In spite of that, somehow, life and Maweu's education continued. He was an extremely bright boy.

It is said that some of the best flowers grow among stones, and it is the miser who knows best the value of money. Maweu was a boy who wanted to do many great things. He loved his mother dearly and dreamt of a time to come when he would clothe her in the finest raiment.

The incident that had robbed Kalunde of her family haunted her wherever she went. She hated and feared this Kaiti, the cruel river that would never tell her where it had taken her four people. Curiously, their bodies were never recovered, although it was unusual for people drowned and carried by flood water to disappear completely. Usually their bodies would be found somewhere, cast up on a bank, however far down the river. Only the bodies of two of the other children were recovered twenty-seven miles away.

Kalunde's home was only half a mile from the river. It seemed to her as if, after the loss of her family, the ground did not yield as much as it had done in former times. But, of course, it wasn't only Kalunde's farm that suffered, though somehow, mysteriously possibly just a coincidence – the deaths of Muthungu, his children and the other seven children, marked the start of a series of famines. It looked as if the sky had become semi-barren. The dry periods became longer, the country was bathed more in red dust and its face grew more bald day by day.

Too often, water became scarce. Either the rains returned for a few days and poured disproportionately then disappeared or they came intermittently after the plants which had grown after the previous rains had already dried. Of course, every time there was a deluge, the efficient drainage called Kaiti guided the water swiftly to the Indian Ocean.

After a few days, Kyandumbi was again a dry village, and the wind began to beat dust from the ground.

Damn Fate!

The people started digging again into the sand, sometimes going down as much as fifteen feet in search of water which would, in any case, last for only a few more weeks before drying up. Then the women would have to start going miles and miles away for a single gourd of water.

Always when the season of Kalunde's loss came round again, especially when the strong wind began to blow, beating up the hill, when the clouds sulked and the scent of wild blooms hung heavy, when the *ngalatumia* were crowned with ripe red berries and the thunderstorm began to respond to the flashes of lightning, times when the earth began to smell of a tomorrow's rain . . . ah, finally when Kalunde felt thirsty, the old grief returned to her in violent waves. Her heart ached with anguish, her tears fell once again. She never quite accepted the loss. She acted and carried herself about as if the lost family had gone on a long safari, and would one day come back.

When the same season returned and everything began to play back in her mind, she did her best to keep herself away from the sight of those ugly rocks in the Kaiti. Too often, she had cursed this river, especially when she was crossing it, going to Nunguni and recrossing it in the evening dog-tired, her muscles screaming for a moment to relax and stretch out. Usually she returned from Nunguni with an aching back. She never crossed this river without thinking about her lost family.

She seemed to build up more fear about the river year after year and wished that one day she could sell the land she had there and buy another plot elsewhere, very far from the Kaiti. Of late, her fear had developed a new intensity. Perhaps it had dug deeper into her subconscious. These days, so often in her dreams, her husband would appear to her carrying Kalolia, her daughter, and standing by the door, he would call out loudly, 'Kalunde!'

'Yes!' she would answer, unable to produce a good voice, loud enough for his hearing.

'Do you hear me?' he would shout.

'Yes!'

'Do you hear me, Kalunde!'

'Yeees!' she would cry.

Then he would say, 'Have I not told you to come down the river with us, at least half-way?'

'No, I will not,' she returned. 'I can't because Maweu is not yet back home.'

By the time she had said that sentence, Muthungu would be going down already, calling out with an echoing voice, 'Maweu! Maweu! Maweu . . .!' The echoes were long and rather metallic, and they faded out with the disappearance of Muthungu. At that point, Kalunde would wake up suddenly, sweating profusely.

After the dream had come to her on three or four consecutive nights, she went all the way to Pastor Joana Mawia, three miles away, to let him pray for her and drive away those spirits. After the prayers, the dream did go away for a long time, although in the long run it traced its way back to her.

Finally, Silvesta Maweu pulled through his school certificate exam. He passed remarkably well in spite of the hardship, securing a First Division. But this time, he was forced to put a full stop to his education so that he could help his ageing mother. Although she had married Muthungu at a very early age, she hadn't given birth until she had lived with him for nearly ten years, when they had given up all hope of ever getting a child. She had conceived Maweu in her early forties.

Kalunde had been lucky in the sense that she was able to marry a young man she loved. Muthungu was a remarkable traditional dancer who usually held the spectators in thrall as he flung and broke and coiled himself as though he had no bones when dancing the curve dances, and acquired the bones when sprinting and springing about with lightning movements.

In the early part of the year after Maweu left school, he made himself the busiest young man in Kyandumbi by working on the farm, determined to revive everything: he made the garden clean, trimmed the dry leaves of the banana plantation and cultivated around the trees. Meanwhile, he was also making himself bricks, first intending to build a house for himself. But as soon as the bricks were ready, he changed his mind and built his mother a better house, then pulled down the old one which, in any case, would have stood on its walls only for another one or two years.

What a good change for Kalunde! What a triumph after a struggle of more than twenty years!

'You know, Mother,' Maweu told her one Christmas Eve. 'I must find myself a job in the new year.'

'You could rest for a year or so.' She looked into his eyes, seeing Muthungu's image in him. 'Until you have finished your own house. There's no hurry, son.'

'There should be hurry,' replied Maweu. He was an impatient young man. 'I think it wouldn't be a bad idea for me to get married quite soon, once I have found a job. I need somebody to help you. I'm interested in a wife who can live with you here while I work, one who can lend me the best hand in upgrading and keeping this farm. She could raise chickens and do many other things that would, with my help, put this home in a better shape. That's what I want, Mother.'

Good fortune came to the young man in the new year, shortly after he had finished grass-thatching his own house. Someone called him up for a job immediately and he was taken for some local training for six months, then, to his dismay, he was posted to work in Mombasa. He thought Mombasa was too far from his home. Like many people from Kyandumbi, he would have liked to work in Nairobi, only some sixty miles away. However, he was grateful to get the job and he was determined to keep it at all cost. Accountancy seemed to be the right career for him as he liked dealing with figures – Mathematics was his best subject. He came to see his mother every other weekend and was able to engage someone to help her. He found a village woman and employed her to keep the home.

In that same year, Silvesta Maweu met Swastika Nzivele in Mombasa and fell in love with her. Nzivele had been born in Kangundo, Tala, about seventy miles from Kyandumbi. She was exceedingly beautiful.

'These beautiful women are difficult to keep,' commented Wambua, a friend and colleague of Maweu.

'Why?' Maweu felt hurt.

'Well, because they know that they are beautiful and expect their beauty to make up for their shortcomings,' observed Wambua as he smoked his cigarette. He was a married man, much older than Maweu.

'I can't leave her because of that,' Maweu fought back.

'I know. For one thing, it is difficult for a man to leave a beautiful girl. Secondly, it's much more difficult if that pretty face is someone you love. Indeed, she is a very comfortable woman to look at; but you know, the comfort of the heart is a different matter. Not that I want to imply anything negative or positive about Nzivele. Of course, there are beautiful flowers that also smell nice, that are lovely in every respect; the devil is not always ugly, in certain cases, he is very beautiful.'

Swastika Nzivele was twenty-one, fresh and sweet looking, medium in size and figure, with a complexion of the inside of a guava. She had a round, spotless face, rather big eyes which begged for sympathy, plentiful hair on her head and nice even teeth, milk white. When she smiled, she radiated great energy and attractiveness. In other respects, she was a simple girl, still forming her personality. She was raw in many ways, but Silvesta Maweu was prepared to grow and ripen her.

In the early days of their meeting, Nzivele was resistant, either because she thought Maweu was too young, or because she wanted to finish the secretarial training which had brought her to Mombasa and which she had just started. But Maweu's persistent efforts to make her his broke into her heart. She threw all the doors open for him. Once touched deeply, Nzivele was an emotional girl and, with a bit of praise, you could take her many miles away.

'I didn't want to fall in love with you,' she told him one day when they had become deeply in love.

'Why?' He coaxed her side with his finger. She squealed and jerked away from him.

'I wasn't ready for it,' she said and kissed her ice-cream. She licked her lips in a dreamy, self-caressing way. 'I should have liked to work for two years at least after finishing my course.'

'Do I stand in your way?'

'Yes . . . with this thing . . . It has big demands.'

'What thing? That I'm asking for your love?' She swung her head and licked her ice-cream.

'Then what?'

'What do you want from me?'

'That's silly! I want many things from you. I guess all that can be summarised in one thing – marriage.'

'I'm too young, don't you feel that?'

'It's good to be young. What about me – am I sixty?'

'Well . . .' She shrugged her shoulders, heaved a sigh and began to eat her ice-cream seriously; watching the Indian Ocean. It had sounded like a joke to him at first, but her face now bore strong feelings about what she was saying.

Silence put a wedge between them for a while. Maweu's thoughts began wandering. He thought about Kyandumbi, about his school days . . . Next, he was looking at the ancient walls of Fort Jesus. What motive did the Portuguese have in constructing the Fort, he wondered. Was it just for defence, or . . .? He heard Nzivele utter a sigh. He turned to her.

Her eyebrows were knitted against the bright sun, then she ironed them out as if she had opened up everything for him. The chocolate ice-cream made her lips sexy.

'There's nothing too young about you,' he said with difficulty.

'Ah!'

He touched her breast. 'Everything of yours is mature. I didn't leave a part of me behind in coming to you. I don't feel I am making a mistake. Rather, I'd be making a mistake if I didn't . . .'

'Didn't what?'

He slid further down, laid his head on her lap, stretched out his legs and picked up her other hand, then crossed his fingers with hers. He shut his eyes. He could hear the sound of her lips as she ate the ice-cream, still looking out to sea as though waiting to see the answer write itself above the water. However, she wasn't confused. Only afraid . . .

She brought down her mouth and kissed his and winced as if she felt pain. His eyes flew open.

The sun had just climbed over the Kivani Hill, so it was about nine in the morning, a gorgeous Sunday morning. The triumph of Silvesta Maweu had brought him home with his charming Nzivele, for the first time, to introduce her to his mother. This morning they were taking a walk towards Koola Town. The romance of this morning was mirrored everywhere.

The air smelt fresh. The gardens were a sea of deep green plants. The beans from whose stalks the white and pink flags of flowers danced in the breeze, as if they were the living tails of the plants, were enchanting. The sound of bees working in the field filled the air. Perhaps this year there would be a good harvest, at least, if the rains continued this way, for there are many abortive seasons in the life of a farmer, especially when the heavens decide to bring no more rain at the very time when the young plants need water.

The couple walked silently together, as if listening to every sound around them. Birds sang, darted and courted joyfully in the air. The hills, the Kilungu range, the Mbooni, the Kiuu, the Muumandu and the Kiimakiu, which surrounded this beautiful location, stood out strongly today. They looked bold and untouched, unaffected by man's endeavours. Everything always looked so heavy and rich after a night of rainfall had beaten down every bit of dust from the trees, repolishing everything. It seemed possible to smell everything, every flower, every herb and the green grass. The banana leaves fluttered dramatically in the wind, tearing into a thousand flags. Voices came from a distance. The young couple heard the crying and calling of children and women from far away, the bleating of goats and sheep, the mooing of cows and the crowing of cocks.

'The sky is so blue today,' Nzivele observed. 'One day I'd like to fly above those clouds. It must be quite an experience.'

'When will that be?'

'Next year perhaps. I could fly from Mombasa to Nairobi . . .

Hey, you know what?' He paused dramatically. 'I know when.'

'When?' Nzivele said teasingly.

'During our honeymoon . . . Oh my!' He kissed her fingers and spun completely round.

'It would be very expensive.' She could not suppress the excitement in her voice.

'It can't be all that expensive.'

'Flying must be scaring.' She cast a look across the sky, then on the country. 'It's beautiful here, Maweu, though drier than Kangundo with all that coffee . . . You have a severe water problem here.'

'Don't mention that,' he said, displeased that the idea of flying hadn't stuck in her mind long. 'We were talking about flying on our honeymoon.'

'We'll talk about that when it comes and when you have the money.'

'What do you want us to talk about now – water? Yes, water is a luxury commodity here, unfortunately. Imagine what one could do with this land if there was enough water for irrigation.'

'How do your people manage?'

'There are bits of water here and there which dry up fast. You should see what happens to the young toads when the water is drying up.' He studied her face. 'Are you terribly disappointed about loving someone from a dry area?' Without waiting for an answer he rushed on enthusiastically, 'The first thing I'll do when I have good money is to build an iron-roof and buy a water tank. I know what it is to live without water. All civilisations begin with water on good land. The land is good here, what we don't have is the water; of course, we forget that a lot of water is always coming and running away. The heavens burst open and pour down all that water, but it is all wasted because it runs back to the ocean immediately.

The technology of harvesting water is all that we need in this place. The rest will be smooth . . . Nzivele,' he worried, 'I hope you'll bear the drought with us when it comes. The place can sometimes be impossible. '

'Don't exaggerate things.' She tried to comfort him.

'You have grown up here and here you are with your girl.''

'I'm glad you understand that.' He squeezed her hand in his.

'I can live anywhere in the world as long as there is love for me.'

'That's good.'

'Tell me something Maweu,' she said, gripping his hand. 'Can I be sure . . . '

'Yes, go on.'

'Well . . . ' she hesitated.

At that moment they branched into a path from the road which would lead them to Koola Town. I think you should walk in front of me,' Maweu suggested. 'The path is too narrow for side-by-side walking. There is something exciting about you from the back.'

'What?'

'That's my secret.'

'Silvesta!' She stopped and looked pleadingly at him. 'I'm ugly from the back, I know.'

'How do you know that? You don't have front mirrors to see your back. Mark you, nobody sees his own back. Your beauty is the apple of other people's eyes, not yours. I can assure you that you look wonderful from the back.'

'Maybe in the front but certainly not from the back.'
'Okay, I'll let you believe what you want. You wanted to ask me something.'

'I know,' she said softly, bearing herself elegantly in front of him, balancing her delightful figure over the uneven ground, her bottom making comfortable gestures. He loved her rounded shoulders. Today she wore a pretty blue dress, with guinea-fowl spots. She had unplaited her hair the previous night and she had combed it very well this morning. It was luxuriant, black hair that looked like a wig, shining with hair oil. Her delicate hands dangled at her sides. Once in a while, she touched her breast in an unconscious self-caress, sighed, then began to hum a tune when silence fell.

'Nzivele,' he called her attention again. 'You wanted to tell me something, or rather, ask.'

'It will upset you.'

'I'm sure it won't.'

'Okay . . .' she hesitated, then stopped and turned to look at him. 'By any chance Maweu, you wouldn't have another girl somewhere around?' She winced as if the thought pained her.

'Yes, I have one – two in fact – more beautiful than you.' He laughed again.

'This is no joke, Silvesta, tell me the truth only.'

'Why, do you think I might be trying to deceive you?'

'You never know men, my mother says. It is usual for boys to have more than one girlfriend at the same time.'

'What about girls?'

'Not as much.'

'They keep at least two, so that if they lose this one, then they can turn to the other. They usually have a second choice. Who is your second choice?'

She thought and replied, 'No one.'

'Why did it take you that long to say, "no one" if there isn't one?'

'My mind was on something else. You have another girl-friend – don't you?'

'Want to give me one?'

'No'

'The best thing is not for me to tell you whether or not I have another one. In the long run, you'll know the truth. I'll ask you to listen more to the sound of my voice and the beat of my heart. I don't want to tell you big words that mean nothing.'

He walked behind her proudly, like a cock following a hen, watching her steps, projecting both his and her image into the future. She wore white shoes and her black hand-bag was slung from her shoulder. He thought she tied her belt too tightly into her waist. At that moment, he wondered what their first child would be. Like all men, he thought he would like to have a son for his first child, whom he would name after his father, Muthungu. What name would he give to the child if it was a daughter?

'Magdalene,' he said to himself, not because he had any important person to honour with that name; he just liked it. Sometimes he thought he should give Nzivele that name too. It was such a lovely name.

'Nzivele,' he touched her shoulder. 'You'll not believe it, but I have only you for myself. You came to my life too quickly before I could see other girls.'

'I hope you'll not start seeing them later when you have become sober from this love.'

'I have grown up to trust my own person and believe in my choices. Even if I don't know exactly where I am going, I can feel the direction. I know I'm on the right path.'

Three women passed them hurriedly, barefoot. All looked rough, bearing the trademark of country life. They carried with them a rather unpleasant smell. But Silvesta Maweu understood it all well. It all boiled down to the same thing – water. To take a bath weekly was for anyone living in this area a luxury. But then, Maweu thought, at this time, with good water around, why should anyone stink?

A cyclist came down the path, concentrating seriously on the zigzag path, looking as tense and worried as if the bicycle was bearing him away against his will. Only when he passed them did they see that he was carrying a child.

'What plant is that which smells so wonderful?'

Nzivele stopped and sniffed. 'Mmh! Can you smell it?'

'Yes,' Maweu answered. 'It's that one over there.'

He pointed at a big blossom.

'What do you call the tree?' she asked.

He thought. 'Sorry, I have forgotten,' he replied.

The *muama* were thick with large leaves. Deep green mango trees showed up on every farm you looked at. A half-naked young boy stood a little way from the path, keenly admiring the looks and cultured elegance of the couple. The sound of the billy-goats, one young, one elderly, courting two females gave further life to the surroundings. Maweu thought about the previous night and the romance of that morning when both were taking their *Jogoo* porridge for breakfast from the same plate, each feeding the other. He thought of the egg that Nzivele had peeled, bitten in half and put one half in Maweu's mouth, saying, 'They will become one flesh and eat with one spoon.'

These small, small things, Maweu thought, are very important in life.

Finally, they emerged into Koola Town which, with its few shops had nevertheless appeared big, rich, and exciting in the days of his childhood, especially on the market day when the women came to trade their commodities, all talking and drowning the place with noise that blended with that of goats, cows, sheep and chickens being sold. The place looked so poor and pathetic now that Maweu had been exposed to other well-developed places. The red brick shops looked more red today, like open wounds. There were a few clusters of women here and there, selling either five or ten bananas, a few onions, some green oranges and small stacks of tomatoes. The women lacked life, giving the impression of shadowy transit traders. Perhaps it wasn't the selling of these items which would, in any case, fetch only two or five shillings, that had brought the women here, but the company of being among other women.

'This is our city,' Maweu told his girlfriend. 'You like it?' He looked at her. 'You don't, I can see that on your face.'

'You are not responsible for its looks, why be sarcastic about it? I have seen other places worse than this – do I come from Europe?'

'It's good to have people like you who understand things. We shouldn't run away from reality; no one can run away from his nudity except by clothing himself. A day may come when all this shame may be covered.'

'Shame?'

'I'm sure you know what I mean, Nzivele.'

'Yes, but I don't see this as shame. Poverty is not a shame; it is a natural fact.'

'That we must put up with?' he challenged her.

'If you are born poor, all you can do is to look for a means of fighting against that situation, but without shame.'

'You think beautifully, my love.'

'Thank you.' She glowed with pride.

'I would like you to have a look at what the women are selling – hardly anything.'

'What? I know what they are selling – what do you think?' she talked knowingly. 'Whether each woman comes here to sell a single potato or pawpaw, that is immaterial. It's a place for meeting others like herself.'

'Correct, Nzivele. If you are poor, you make friends with poor people. They'll tell you how to bear poverty, how to eat a few grains of maize without beans washed down with a mug of water, yet go out smiling to life. Pastor Joana Mawia – you haven't met him yet – says that there is always something to smile for even when you are in prison.'

'Who's this Pastor?'

'A family friend of ours. I'd like us to pay him a visit this afternoon, it's not far from our house.'

Nzivele took a second glance round the shops. 'So this is your Koola Town?'

'Yes, our city, with no street names.'

She laughed.

'Laughing at poverty?'

'No. Laughing at the city with no street names. I don't laugh at poverty, anybody can be poor.'

Just as she finished saying so, a drunkard popped out from one of the shops, staggering and shouting out crude curses.

'Let's hurry up,' Maweu grabbed her hand. 'That drunkard knows me and he'll start a scene if he sees me. This town, sadly, produces more drunkards than the items sold in the shops. See that one over there?'

'Why are there so many of them?' she asked, frowning.

'I don't know,' he replied, hesitating. The first drunkard stood outside the shops, his trunk swaying like a tree in the wind, his bad sight trying to decipher who the couple were. His trousers, red like the earth, were patched over in green, blue, check, red – any colour, yet the clubs of his knees showed through other holes. His jacket, nearly as torn as the leaf of a banana, must have been oversized when he got it. The left-hand pocket was wet with an egg that had broken inside it.

'Why do they drink like this?' Maweu pondered aloud. 'I suppose there are so many of them here, drinking like this because they don't know what to do with themselves. There's nothing else to do, only drinking and sex.' He shrugged his shoulders. 'So what to do?'

Nzivele had to agree. It seemed as if everywhere she looked, her eyes met another drunkard. All of them looked the same – sunken cheeks, a hard and dusty head planted on a thin frame – quite a number of young men in their thirties already looking about seventy.

'Thank God there are no women drunkards,' he said.

'Women are much more sensible,' she teased him. 'Look round, what do you see? The women I see here are decent, walking straight. What on earth is this disease with men?'

'One of them said he drinks like that because his wife *sits* too much on him.'

Occasionally a thin dog trotted past with its rump not quite following the front legs as if it was being blown faster by wind. A bitch, not comfortable to look at, passed with her long, loose dugs swaying, sniffing everywhere, looking for anything to eat which might keep her alive after the relentless sucking by her litter of puppies. Other thin dogs circled, looking for bones, some courting, charging and snarling at their rivals.

'You don't have to look at the drunkards and the dogs,' Maweu said defensively, as if both were his children of whom he was ashamed. 'Don't look at the dust and the rest, look at the people like ourselves, and the beautiful mountains. Don't you worry, though, in a few years time, some of these drunkards will be dead and this place will be a nice town, with named streets, healthy people and good trade.'

'When will that be?'

'God is great, you know.'

The drunkard whom they had first seen cut across the road and staggered towards them.

'Hey, you man!' Maweu cursed. 'I don't want to talk to you, go!'

'*Aah, Mwanaa Muthungu, we!*' The drunkard opened his mouth wide exposing his rusty teeth, half-smiling, half-serious, saliva drooling. He paused a few feet from Maweu and addressed him in broken English, 'Wat youaaa . . . son of Muthungu . . . Me know much you.'

'Leave us alone,' Maweu said politely and pulled at Nzivele's arm. 'Let's go.' Maweu kept Nzivele busy with answering questions while he steered her quickly away.

Two men crossed in front of Maweu and Nzivele, chasing after a chicken. One of the dogs caught sight of the good game and joined the men in the chase, hoping that when the chicken was slaughtered, he would be given, at least, the intestines to eat. Meat was precious here. People ate the chicken completely, even the head and the legs and crunched the bones for the marrow.

It was not a market day, otherwise the place would have been filled with the noise of the country women, selling cassava, dry beans, sour milk, bananas, green leaves, pots, secondhand clothes, sisal ropes and straps, oranges, chickens, goats and cows, millet, snuff and so on – a lively and colourful sight.

'I like the place in spite of everything,' Nzivele said, looking at her white shoes which were already full of dust. 'Honestly, I don't see only the drunkards and the thin and wretched dogs, but other, nice people.'

Maweu felt better at this. He chose a fairly well-stocked shop and invited her to go in. 'Come, let's have a Coke here. The people here are friends . . . What counts most in life is what people are at heart, not what clothes they wear. This is going to be your city – what do you think?'

'What will be the name of this street?'

'Mulandi. Mother talks of Mulandi who was a brave man from these parts, a famous warrior. He's been dead for a long time now.'

They entered the shop holding hands, which caused some sensation among the locals who always considered it funny for a man to walk holding hands with a woman as if she was either a walking stick or was sick. Many eyes followed them as they went into the shop. Meanwhile, a coal black, short woman with a disturbed mind waded her way through the other people and came face to face with Maweu, almost bumping into him.

'*Mwalimu*, give me a ten cent to buy some scones.' He gave her a shilling and she was all smiles. Everybody here seemed bent on making him feel uncomfortable, he thought worriedly, what was Nzivele going to think? If he had magic to change things, he would cast a spell, make the place a modern town and bury all these shameful people. It is a good feeling when the girl you are wooing from a far place admires your village, its people and development. When someone tells you that you come from a backward location, you feel the pinch. That's hurtful.

'Nzivele,' he whispered in her ear. 'What will you take?' His feet were sweating in his shoes. Everyone seemed to be staring at the couple.

'I think I'll take Sprite.'

'I too.' He pulled her to himself as if fearing some one else would claim her. Their eyes met. Nzivele liked drinking from the same bottle as her lover. She checked round to see who was looking at them that moment. Everybody! City people were always some kind of curiosity to country ones.

Maweu felt as tired as if he had walked twenty miles. This coming had not been a planned one; he would have liked the chance to make better preparations for bringing Nzivele to his home. Then, possibly, he could have planned every move and decided on which people they should see. But he had got a letter from his mother informing him that she was sick, so it was mainly her illness which had brought him here. Nzivele had asked to come with him and he had agreed. It would be an opportunity for his mother to see this girl Nzivele he had talked to her about.

Maweu and Nzivele returned home before three. He was impressed by her appreciation of many things which he would have thought otherwise were bad and awkward. She had boosted his confidence greatly.

'Home is where love is;' was her verdict on the day.

4

◆ ◆ ◆ ◆

The marriage didn't take place all that quickly. Maweu and Nzivele were married nine months after he had taken her to Koola for the first time. It was a big and successful wedding that brought fifty people from Kangundo in a hired bus to attend. Nzivele's father, Shadrak Mbalu, who had just received his coffee money, contributed generously to the wedding. Mbalu had a thousand coffee plants which were quite good, by local standards. Nzivele was his last child. His three sons were already working in Nairobi and the daughter whom Nzivele followed was studying on a scholarship in America. So Shadrak Mbalu could afford to give Nzivele what she wanted.

Pastor Joana Mawia married them at Makutano African Inland Church. The wedding cake, the first of its kind ever to be seen in Kyandumbi, had been ordered from Nairobi. The third tier of the cake, unfortunately, had broken during the jumps and dances of the car crossing the ditches off Kitandi, leading to Kyandumbi.

'You know,' pronounced an elder at the wedding, 'it's a bad omen for a wedding cake to break before it is cut.'

But that wasn't the way Nzivele had seen it. On seeing the broken cake and hearing the words of the omen, she had replied, 'Did you people really expect that a delicate cake would withstand all those bumps miraculously?'

Then the story began. It was six months after their wedding day. Maweu took some leave and came home to set up something for Nzivele. The idea of keeping chickens and developing the farm was something she liked.

This was all joy for Kalunde who had never been so happy in her life. She had loved Nzivele right from the beginning. To begin with, the two were the closest of friends. Kalunde had cried real tears during the sermon that Pastor Joana Mawia had given on her son's wedding day.

'We'll be rich soon,' Nzivele said, delighted with the farming plan. 'I must grow coffee too, then I'll be the first person around to grow coffee. This soil looks just as good as that we have in Kangundo; coffee could do very well here.'

Maweu built a shelter for the chickens, bought thirty-five local birds to start with, plastered his house and painted it. Before returning to Mombasa, he left six hundred shillings with Nzivele to take on someone to tidy up the garden and dig holes for planting coffee for the next season, as she had requested.

About a year later, Kalunde's life had improved appreciably. At any age, success is always welcomed and good. The old woman shed the scales and feathers of old age and put on weight. She looked younger, ten years younger. The pride was hers that, as everybody said, her son had brought home an industrious and wise wife who loved not only her husband but the husband's mother. Meantime, Maweu continued coming home every other weekend.

'A wise wife,' people told Kalunde, 'is a great gift, and an industrious wife is the light of the home.'

'Praise the Lord,' was all Kalunde could say to this. She had discovered that Nzivele responded extremely well to praises, so she praised the girl for everything she did. And Nzivele tried her best to deserve the praise. Theirs wasn't really like the relationship of a daughter-in-law and a mother-in-law, but more like that between a mother and her own daughter.

Eggs started arriving, chicks, friends and blessing. The church elders and Christian friends paid frequent long visits to their home and they held long discussions there about their faith and the coming of civilisation. Nzivele had become a church woman. Wherever she went, she radiated energy.

'Wife is the home and husband is the house.' People confirmed the old saying as they observed Nzivele's marriage to this home.

'Poverty ripens old age and affluence delays it,' the villagers said about Kalunde's former and new figure.

There were two men working in the garden already, in preparation for growing coffee. Nzivele engaged a third man. 'My husband and I want to put up something decent here,' she told the man. 'I want ten thousand bricks.'

In two years' time, they intended to put up a five bedroomed house, a barn, a separate kitchen and a bigger shed for the increasing number of chickens. A house of the size they planned would, with the water tanks Maweu wanted, to supply them with more than enough water for their needs. They also planned to start a plant nursery.

But the plant nursery was never started, for the house was never put up. The bricks were made and the five kilns built, but they were never fired. This was partly because the servant had not been paid his salary for the last two months, partly because there was no money for the firewood and partly because things had gone wrong somewhere. Even the coffee holes were never finished . . .

The gatherings and the many friends drifted away, as rapidly as they had come . . . Nzivele stopped going to the church.

A bitter disagreement had arisen between Kalunde and Nzivele, rooted in a recent event. Nzivele had invited some friends to her house for an evening meal. After the meal, there had been a dance that went on until two in the morning. Maweu wasn't present. Things wouldn't have been too bad, perhaps, if Kalunde Muthungu had not seen, among the friends, a Simon Mosi who, the gossips said, had been seen a number of times around Kalunde's home. But the rumours had gone deeper than that. They said Simon Mosi and Nzivele had been seen somewhere, somehow, misbehaving.

Kalunde had tried to sit on the dance affair. But the more she sat on it, the more the lid burnt her. Then she decided to ask Nzivele about it.

'Ng'aMbalu.' Kalunde often called Nzivele after her father's name. 'The dance of yours . . .'

'Yes!' Nzivele had been interrupted while she was sipping her afternoon tea. She put the cup down slowly.

'Yes, what about it?'

Kalunde thought for a while, realising how heavily she had hit home at Nzivele.

'What about it?' Nzivele was impatient.

'You don't think your husband would question it?'

'Why should he?'

'Well . . .' Kalunde hesitated.

'What do you want to imply by that, Mother?'

'What would I want to imply, child? My sole interest is that you and your husband should live happily, without mis-understandings and continue to bless Muthungu's home.' She cleared her throat and spat the mucus a few yards from her. Both women were seated outside the house under a mango tree.

'Ng'aMbalu, we have a name which we must maintain.' Kalunde broke the silence.

'Any rise is harder to achieve than a fall . . .'

Nzivele sipped her tea carefully and stayed silent for a while, with a knitted brow. One could see many shades of emotion coming and passing over that face. She suspected rightly that Kalunde was going to touch on something about Mosi. It was true that Simon Mosi had flirted with her. In fact, he did so every time he met her.

She grunted. Kalunde came in from another angle.

'Ng'aMbalu, it looks as if I shouldn't have asked you that.'

Nzivele cleared her throat and answered, 'I didn't know I was being watched.' She sighed, and pretended to be calm.

'Watched?' Their eyes met.

'It looks . . .' she put the tea on one side and started biting her nails, spitting soundly.

'Nobody is watching you the way you seem to have taken it – nobody.'

'Then why did you ask me that question?' She was bold.

'Because I care about how people talk of it.'

'Talk?' Nzivele winced.

'Yes, I said so.'

'What would they talk about?' Nzivele's body stirred, heat building up from within.

'Ng'aMbalu, everybody admires you here. I don't have to tell you that a good name walks with many eyes.'

'What are they saying?'

'You are my kingpost,' Kalunde pursued her original thought.

There was silence between them.

'I wouldn't like to hear a bad word uttered about you, Ng'aMbalu but I can't close my eyes and ears.'

'But what have you heard; what have you seen?'

Nzivele crossed her hands over her breast.

'Nothing,' Kalunde said, after a long time.

'Nothing?'

'Child, not everyone who comes to pay you a visit comes to bless you, consider that point.'

'What does that mean?'

'Does an adult goat bleat for nothing?'

'Then why are you hiding what you have heard from me?'

Kalunde stayed silent, looking away, wondering how she could put across this delicate subject without hurting Nzivele deeply. It was a dilemma. Would sitting on it heal it? But talking about it would, or it might blow things up. It was a gamble. It can hurt you if you wound the donkey that carries you on its back. These days, Kalunde realised that Nzivele carried her.

'My labour is not appreciated,' Nzivele's temper began to boil and spurt, 'only the bad things are noticed. '

'You know how much I have appreciated you, Ng'aMbalu. Everybody knows that. What is Kalunde without you?'

'Don't cover things up, Mother.'

'What do you want me to say?'

'What you have heard people say about me, and what you think might have taken place at the dance . . .' she began to stammer.

'You don't have the strength for carrying what you are asking Ng'aMbalu.'

'I don't talk in riddles,' Nzivele was angry.

'Yes, I know that. But I know you do know that nudity is left in the bedroom.'

'What do you mean, Mother?'

There was a very long silence between them. The atmosphere was explosive. Nzivele made efforts to rise and return to her house, but her limbs refused to obey her. She wished that a neighbour would drop in to break the tension. Panic seized her.

Makenzi, the dog, lay by the door on his side, breathing in deep draughts as if he was listening to everything being said.

Nzivele continued angrily, 'People say that you shouldn't try to cover up a fire with a cloth . . . It would be better if you could come straight out with what you know – say it to my face – I'm sure it can't kill me.'

'I mentioned the dance,' Kalunde said with difficulty, 'because I thought it would create misunderstanding.'

'What misunderstanding?' Nzivele's face was bitter.

'Do I have to tell you that you are a married woman?'

'Don't I know that already?'

'Very well. But that is not what I mean.'

'Then say what you mean!' Nzivele wanted to terminate this argument, yet her conscience wouldn't let her. Her questions came out automatically.

'They have started saying that you are falling a prey to bad men - is that what you want to hear?'

'Who's saying that, Maweu?'

'What answer will you have for him when he comes?'

Nzivele heaved a sigh, and the words poured out, heavy with sarcasm. 'I'll tell him about the dance and whom you think is seducing me.'

'We should close this subject now, Ng'aMbalu.'

'Because you have succeeded in giving me the bruise you wanted, that's quite clear.'

'Never in my heart, I suck your feet.'

More damaging words followed. 'You should have told me straight to my face that you didn't like some of the people I invited. I know that – I'm smarter than you think.'

'I don't doubt that.'

'There are people you don't like.'

'Such as?' Kalunde found another opening.

'Do I know? You are the one who knows them.' However long the argument continued, the name Simon Mosi remained unspoken, although both Kalunde and Nzivele knew that he was at the back of everything: the invisible guest.

Like a butterfly that had been handled roughly and made to shed its beauty, Nzivele's enthusiasm was destroyed by that talk, that argument, that fight with Kalunde. Her heart froze and finally became a stone towards the old woman.

Grief fell into Kalunde's life. To start with, Nzivele began to cook her own meals in her own house, stopped paying the servants in an attempt to send them away and stopped giving Kalunde any help. She shed her old diplomatic way of talking to Kalunde and became rough and hard. She cursed the pets loudly and began to sing provocative songs around her house. Now, when she sneezed, she did so proudly, then coughed and spat mockingly. The food she gave to Kalunde was tough, roughly cooked maize with a countable number of bean grains that Nzivele herself hadn't eaten.

But worse had yet to come, even more bitter things. Eventually, Nzivele got rid of the chickens, selling those she thought should be sold and eating the others. She began to frequent Mombasa with bodily complaints that were mysterious to doctors. One day she complained of stomach pains, the next it was either pains in the kidney, or the pelvis, or the chest, or the back. One thing led to another. Maweu was taken by surprise; it made him feel stupid. He started worrying himself sick about his mother's health.

'We are going to kill my mother,' he told Nzivele the time she was in Mombasa for treatment and was reluctant to return to the country.

'How?' Nzivele asked innocently, as if she didn't know what he meant.

'How? Who's taking care of her?'

'What about my health?' she said defensively. 'You shouldn't make such remarks. Have I not been taking care of her? Have I not been carrying your mother on my back for nearly two years? Are you now trying to teach me how to love her? As long as I lived for her in good health, all was fine . . . let my health . . . or let something bad happen to my health and there I am – I'm now of no value. My body has blood, not water, just as your mother's. Ah, what a terrible thing life is!'

'Nzivele, this is no way to talk. I didn't say you were going to kill Mother. I said we. Why do you defend yourself like that?'

She attacked him from another angle. 'If I had a child to occupy me, you wouldn't . . .'

'No, no, no!' he cut her short. 'We are not going to discuss child problems here. A child comes from God and if He doesn't want you to have one, there's very little you can do.'

'A lot can be done about it, don't forget,' she pressed.

'How?'

'We are seeing the wrong doctors.'

'What senseless talk is this?' He heated up. 'Are you often sick like this because you don't have a child?'

'You think of nobody else but your mother.'

'Talk straight!' Maweu shouted and stood up. She was lying in bed, wrapped up in a white sheet, leaving only her face on view. It was already after midnight and Maweu had wanted to go to bed early. He looked round the single-roomed flat as if his eyes were following a flying insect.

'I can go home to die there, if that would please you.' Nzivele turned her back on him and started talking to the wall. 'I didn't come for pleasure, I came because I am sick.'

'How does the child argument come into it? How many years is it since we were married - ten? Two, just two years, and here you are already worrying yourself to death!'

'I'm sick, I'm not trying to kill your mother.'

'I don't like the way you refer to her these days, *your mother*. Why do you do that?'

'If you think that I'm not good enough for her, engage another person to take care of her.'

'So that you could quarrel and make trouble with the person and finally dismiss him?'

'I . . .' She turned to face him. 'I must be a devil in your eyes!'

Maweu could see that his mother was suffering. She had lost a lot of weight and become silent. Could Nzivele bluff him any more that she was really taking care of his mother?

But Kalunde, too, sat on the matter. She wouldn't talk to her son about what was happening. For one thing, she feared that if she told him the truth about his wife's behaviour, he would take it out on Nzivele very roughly, or possibly start thinking of divorcing her. Whenever Maweu asked her about Nzivele's behaviour, Kalunde did her best to avoid answering the questions by going round the subject or treating it lightly.

Soon, however, she wouldn't be able to keep it a secret any more. People had already started openly talking about it. They said that Nzivele had been 'bitten by a tsetse fly'.

Kalunde now went down to the river to draw her own water, she fetched her own firewood, cooked her own meals, swept the house and sat in it, lonely. But she made her son believe that Nzivele was still doing everything for her. Meanwhile, even when in Kyandumbi, Nzivele ate as richly as her heart wished. She had everything: meat, rice, eggs, bread, jams, honey, vegetables, milk – the full list. And she had money with her, always. Kalunde's health was obviously not good; but Nzivele would never help her even by washing the clothes. Rather, she added another pinch to the pain. When her husband sent money to be given to Kalunde, Nzivele pocketed it and went completely silent to see what other powers Kalunde had. Things went from bad to worse. Nzivele had pulled down nearly everything.

One evening, Kalunde sat down for hours desperately trying to chew her food, which was the usual maize and a few beans. At the same time she was chewing over the mental distress of her life of late. She broke into tears at last for she had so few teeth in her mouth that eating such stuff was almost impossible. On that particular evening she wished that death would take her away. She had lost grip of Nzivele completely, who sometimes disappeared for days. Either Nzivele would wake up in the morning and go away, nobody knew where, and return home quietly by dark, or she went to Machakos, then to Kangundo to visit her parents. Whatever she did, Nzivele had managed to raise an aura of mystery about herself.

Early one morning Kalunde woke up and decided to go to talk about it to somebody she could trust, Pastor Joana Mawia, the man who had always been an inspiration to her life. Always, the pastor seemed to know what to tell everybody to heal their worries. His words and his prayers soothed and relieved. He was close to sixty, younger than Kalunde.

As she walked, Kalunde realised that her energy was betraying her. She felt hungry and light-headed; her saliva that morning had tasted bitter, as if she had licked the milk of an aloe. Was malaria going to strike and finish her off? Her stomach was upset, possibly because of the indigestible grains that she had tried to eat the previous night, breaking each grain two or three times, then swallowing. She had eaten the few beans that there were and drunk water from her little gourd that barely carried a pint. She could hardly remember when last she had taken a bath.

In the bygone days of friendship, Nzivele always warmed water for Kalunde's bath, and even washed her back. From time to time also, the two had sat outside the house while Nzivele cut and filed Kalunde's nails lovingly as they enjoyed a conversation on many things. The girl had washed Kalunde's underwear and made her beautiful finger-millet porridge in the morning with lemon and sugar. Her art showed in cooking.

But times had changed. Today Nzivele had withdrawn all those favours. Kalunde wore her clothes until they were stiff with dirt. Lice found a good home in her. Rats returned to her house and fleas as well.

Unless a neighbour dropped in, the old woman would spend hours sitting under the mango tree when the sun was hot, or basking in the morning and evening sunshine. Always with her outside was her friend Makenzi, sitting or lying nearby. Occasionally the two would exchange gestures as a means of communication. Lately Makenzi had discovered that he was no longer a friend of Nzivele. The last beating from her had left him with no doubt that she had become an enemy. She had hit him so hard with the back of a hoe that he had spent over a month recovering from the attack. Since then, he had kept his distance from her.

Earlier on, Kalunde had had another friend, too, a cat who had also been a friend of Nzivele's until the girl had declared her cold war on Kalunde. Since then Nzivele had renamed the cat 'Kalunde', firstly because the cat had once eaten a piece of meat of hers and secondly because Kalunde seemed to love the cat more than ever. One evening, Nzivele gave the cat a fatal blow on the neck with the blunt edge of a panga. Three weeks later, she poisoned Makenzi.

A mile away from her home, Kalunde took a break from her walk to Joana Mawia. She lowered her old body slowly and sat, her knees cracking. She cast a look across the country. Everything was dry and depressing. The valleys and the temples of the Kilungu Hill, the gorges and the bare ridges, looked like parts of a dying earth.

'God' she murmured, 'why do you make it so good sometimes, then take it away and give grief in return?'

She held her head between her hands and said a prayer for Nzivele and her son . . . that they should come to understand their responsibilities and return to the right path. 'Lord, call me back home so that I don't continue to be a burden to these young ones,' she prayed.

She concluded the prayer and looked round again, seeing imaginary flashing forms that started like dots, then grew and spread out like bats, after which they vanished. She shook her head to get rid of them. What could be causing them, she wondered.

This prayer that God should take her life was not her first one. It was now over a year since she started praying for release. But the death she wanted didn't come at once. Instead it came in small installments that were painful. Her life stuck to the cavities of her body as both physical and spiritual hunger gnawed her. There is nothing worse, she said to herself, than the poverty of unwantedness, especially when you are old, with no hope of recovery, with no energy to make things better, with only ghosts and death staring at you in the nearby shadows . . .

She thought of her son. How had he felt when he woke that morning? How was he faring with Nzivele?

'Ah,' she said aloud. 'We'll wait and see.' She had said this many times, but without knowing precisely what she meant. From the whirlwind of her mind, she always spoke this sentence aloud. She felt bad because she had failed to woo Nzivele back. She had tried to bend too much towards the girl, even to the extent of trying to imply that she could have her dances and do other things if she wished; but Nzivele was no longer foolish. She knew what she wanted. 'A thief starts by breaking off his friendship with the good people,' Kalunde said to herself.

She tried to get up on her feet, summoning all her remaining energy and finally feeling the cold earth under her bare foot. Maweu had bought her rubber shoes, but she felt stronger and more sure of her steps when she felt the earth under her feet, when her toes could assist in gripping the ground, and not when the whole foot was sheathed in a thing that had corners. She staggered from one side of the path to the other, unaware that she was doing so. Before getting to Mawia's home, there was a final climb. Just then Kalunde discovered that she had made a mistake. Why had she not sent for Pastor Joana Mawia himself to come to see her at her home? Yet perhaps it would be better for Joana to be seated at his home talking to her; it would help him to give her his best. She couldn't expect Joana Mawia would heal her anyway. It was only that when you have to die, it was good to talk to someone, to die with someone you knew by your side, perhaps, someone to take your farewell.

She crossed a small river which had a pool of dirty water nearby, full of all kinds of creatures. She bent and brushed the water with her hand, then applied the wet hand to her face. She felt better in that dead, silent world. It seemed as if she was the only human being living, for she hadn't met any-body on her way, and there was no sound of life anywhere.

Among the things she wanted to talk about with Pastor Joana Mawia was a peculiar, persistent nightmare, that came to torment her frequently these nights as soon as she had fallen asleep. Could it be a development of the other one in which she saw her husband with her daughter?

5

◆ ◆ ◆ ◆

It was clear in Joana Mawia's eyes that this woman was desperately hungry. He refused to listen to her dream before she had eaten something. They sat outside the house against the wall, basking in the morning sun. Meanwhile, Mawia's wife was busy making some porridge for Kalunde.

Three jolly goat kids capered and ran a race round the house. They looked so lively and happy, reminding Kalunde of her younger, happier life. She felt the exhaustion from walking in her knees and ankles. Old age is the most powerful force, she thought, looking across the hill and remembering how she used to devour long distances and yet come home feeling strong. Old age creeps into you silently, secretively, without your slightest knowledge; you just found yourself aching with it one day, just as you once found yourself adult without knowing how you got there, she thought.

'It looks so good!' Kalunde admired the porridge, richly prepared with milk and sugar. It was a long time since she had taken porridge like this. She drained it silently, gratefully, but painfully. At that moment she realised that, in spite of her better nature, she wished that something could happen to her son's wife, Swastika Nzivele, just something – she didn't know what. She cleared her throat and felt the weight of the porridge in her stomach, a good feeling. She felt warmer and her eyesight seemed keener. It had taken her a full hour to climb the hill to Mawia's home. One of the things that had encouraged her to come here was that she was sure she would get some thing to eat from this home.

Hardship and hunger had pushed her eyes back, deep into the sockets. Her lips were dry and cracked; her hands had become rough like the leaves of a pumpkin vine or sand-paper. She had a wound in her left leg, just below the knee. When unprotected, the flies squeezed in rivalry on to the wound, as many I as could fit, until what you saw was like a black patch over the wound. There must have been at least twenty flies feasting on the raw flesh unnoticed unless one of them hit a patch that was more sensitive. Then Kalunde would curse and chase them away before fetching either a leaf or a rug to cover the wound.

'What is this dream of yours?' Pastor Joana Mawia asked. He was a healthy man, with a full face, a full set of teeth, and a few scattered grey hairs on his head. Faith, he said, kept him strong. 'The Lord,' he always emphasised.

'It is the same dream always,' Kalunde said. 'I see all this area.' She pointed at the large valley of River Kaiti, hundreds of square miles wide. 'All this is covered by a lake - very deep water, stretching from up there, down, down, to all that and this area. Then, I don't understand . . . I see my house still down there, it is far under the water. Other times I am in the house in that water but I don't seem to be drowning, just trying to climb up the slippery side of the lake; but I am always falling.

'I cry for help, but does anyone come to my rescue? No. Every person I see seems to be busy doing something. At the side of the lake, all around, I see many people harvesting the heavy crop of millet that seems to cover the entire country. The people are whistling and singing . . ., And I hear voices of women somewhere at the back, thrashing millet joyfully, singing.

'As I look, a colossal bull lifts its head towards Muumandu Hill bellowing; at the same time I hear the ululations of women who are singing and praising the coming of the bull. But I keep on climbing and falling back into the lake.

'I begin to drown!' she concluded, closing her eyes firmly as if trying to bear some unknown pain. 'That's the dream, Joana.'

Joana Mawia thought silently, looking far over Kiimakiu, a frown of concentration on his face as if he was trying to read the interpretation of that dream from that distance. Finally, he shook his head and said, 'I find it a strange dream. But I don't think you should think too much about it.'

'Shouldn't I?' Kalunde questioned. 'It would frighten you to death if it were you dreaming like that.' She smiled, her face ironing out some of the wrinkles and creating more. She beat the flies from her wound.

'To start with, there's no lake here; and never will be one. Nor will there come a time in future when people will return to growing millet so plentifully . . . You are dreaming of the past. Yes, but . . .' He thought again for a while. 'What about the bull? I think the dream is out of proportion . . . Or, I don't know.'

'There's some great symbol in the dream,' Kalunde said, convinced.

'Do you see what it is?'

'Harvest.'

'When?'

'How do I know?'

There was silence between them.

'Perhaps when I'm dead.' Her face lit up. 'When I have drowned – my days are not long now.'

'But what has the harvest to do with you?' Mawia was puzzled.

'That's what I ask myself.'

'Will the people ever go back to growing millet?'

'Harvest is the symbol.'

'Oh I see,' Mawia nodded, though not in agreement with what she was saying. He was only thinking. 'What about the water – the lake? You don't think that it is also a symbol?'

'It could be, but I wonder why I'm drowning in the lake.'

Pastor Joana Mawia was not helpful to Kalunde's dream. It puzzled him just as much as it did Kalunde. Afterwards, she talked to him about her son's wife, and how she herself felt neglected. Then she touched on Nzivele's affair with Simon Mosi. This was the first time she had revealed the matter to him. But Joana Mawia, like many other people of Kyandumbi, knew of this affair and had an idea that something terrible was happening between Nzivele and Kalunde. The entire village talked about the girl.

He wondered whether Nzivele had any knowledge of what people were saying about her behind her back. Not many respectable people went to pay her a visit these days.

'I can see your problem, sister,' the pastor said to Kalunde after listening to her. Then he stared at her as though the problem was a physical one which he could see on her face. 'But . . .' he hesitated. 'Does Maweu know about this? You ought to tell him, just the way you told me. A wound is also painful when you are washing it to treat it. Sometimes things get too desperate before you discover them and start making repairs. But, whatever the reason, you mustn't be silent about this, not any more.'

'I don't want to keep silent about it, but I have to, Joana.'

'Why must you?'

'I know that son of mine. He'd jump on Nzivele . . . I fear what might happen.'

'Don't you also fear what might happen if you keep silent about it?'

'That, too. But I think it is better for him to find out about it after I have gone. I won't last another season.'

'Sister, the distance of death is often difficult to feel.'

'Not at an age like mine . . . I thought I should leave it until he discovers the truth one day.'

'That is not constructive. It is an evil that has entered your home and you should not give it accommodation. Don't let your son eat filth when you are watching.'

'The wife is a stone. I fear what she might do to me when she learns that I have told these things to Maweu.'

'All thieves expect to be found out one day; it is not a surprise when it happens. Your son's wife will be expecting it; she can do nothing to you.'

'The cat went first, then the dog; next it will be me.'

'You've got to discuss these things with him; you can't run away from that responsibility. Indeed, it might return her back to the right path.'

'Maybe . . . '

'Do you think the marriage is stable?'

She shrugged her shoulders. 'You ask me?'

'I have faith that your son wants you to be happy in your old age. You must give him a chance to make your life happy.'

'I carry lots of fears with me, brother. I don't know which way I am going . . . It's as if I'm falling. Maybe this is the meaning of my dream.'

Pastor Joana Mawia found it difficult to advise the deeply disturbed old woman. Later, after reading her a few healing verses from the Psalms, he asked her to pray with him. He didn't feel like saying the prayer in the house or asking his wife to come to join them as he would have done at any other time. He got to his feet slowly, looking certain of his faith in the powers of Jesus Christ. He took off his hat, readied himself, rubbed his hands together, licked his lips, cleared his throat and opened, 'Dear Lord, dear Jesus Christ, we may be rugged in body with old age, but to our Lord, we are small and young children. We may be living or dead, but to you Lord, our God, we are still your children. There is a lot in this life which we cannot understand, but you can understand all. There is much that we can't see because we are blind, but you can see all, everything. This is because you are the light. It is because of this, Lord, that we come to you. I ask you to turn to this child who feels cold because she has no place on earth for her which is warm . . . She comes to you because you are the only answer to life. Lord, it is not good that man should have nothing to eat. Kalunde has been deserted by her only hope. Her daughter-in-law has changed from being a loaf of bread into a stone. Satan has entered her spirit and built a home in her. She was salt; but now she is salt that has lost its taste and become like sand . . . Lord, stretch out your kind hand and let this child live her last days in peace, with food and water to drink. Don't let her suffer. Would it not please you Lord to remove that worm that has entered Maweu's wife that she now considers her mother her enemy? Who can heal all this except you, our Lord?

'Give Kalunde peaceful sleep, Lord, I pray you; and take away that nightmare from her life, for she has suffered. She lost her children and husband many years ago; but she has lived with the hope that her only son will bless her with protection.

'Talk to Nzivele's heart; revive her, Lord. Young people forget that a time will come in their life when they will need the help of their children . . . '

Pastor Joana Mawia concluded his prayer, and Kalunde's shaken voice pronounced the 'Amen' energetically as if the prayer had already come true.

Mawia returned to his seat slowly and sat silently, looking slightly dissatisfied as though he had discovered that some very important words were missing from the prayer.

6

◆ ◆ ◆ ◆

Who was this Simon Mosi?

A young, very handsome man of that name lived across the River Kaiti, so that his home and that of Maweu faced each other, as Nzivele faced him. Mosi's home was higher up from the river than Maweu's such that he could look down at Maweu's as he looked down at Nzivele because he was a tall man.

Simon Mosi smoked heavily to deaden his depression, to 'kill his nerves' as they say. But when he was not gripped by melancholy, he was an extremely pleasant man to talk to. His temperament ruled him – he was a very sensitive man. That may explain why he was constantly having rows with his wife. He was unhappily married, but his unhappiness in marriage could neither be blamed solely on his wife, Nthemba, nor on him. Simon Mosi was a difficult man to live with because of his depressions, but Nthemba was an impatient and dirty wife.

The affair between Simon Mosi and Nzivele had started off very simply. He had met her one afternoon at Koola Town. Of course, they had met many other times on occasions that hadn't left any mark. Nzivele had simply asked for a lift on

Simon Mosi's bicycle one day. 'I'm sure Simon you wouldn't mind giving me a lift on your Rolls Royce.'

'My what?' he had asked laughing.

'Your that.' Nzivele's smiles were always enticing.

'Well, at your own risk I'll give you a lift. Have you ever seen a man and a woman fall off a bicycle?'

'No.' She looked up at him.

'It's an awful sight, especially the way the woman falls. '

'You think we'll fall today?'

'Pardon?' He was thinking about her beauty, not the ride.

'Are you going to fall?'

'You never know.' He noticed a small patch of wetness under her armpit, she must have been sweating, he realised. 'Don't you trust my riding?'

'As long as you are not drunk, yes.'

'I have ridden a bicycle for over ten years, off and on of course, but I have never fallen off. Well . . .' he said, stammering slightly, admiring her cheeks, fair eyebrows and long eyelashes.

'Well – well what?' she pursued.

'When you are through with your shopping, let me know . . . I'll take you.' He smiled.

'Anything strange on my face?' She wiped it.

'Why? Nothing!'

'The way you are looking at me.'

'Oh that? Do you always become nervous when people look at your face?' He laughed, turned away and thought for a while, looking down. When he turned back to her he asked, 'When is Maweu coming home?'

'This coming Saturday. Why?'

'Maybe he could help me to get a job down there.'

'Oh come on, Simon'

'You think I wouldn't take the job?'

'Let's leave that subject.' She started walking. 'Where do I find you when I'm through?'

'Down at the corner. Buying a lot?'

'No, hardly anything to put in a basket – I'm broke.'

'You are?'

He jumped on the bicycle and rode a way, in a rather swaying style.

Simon Mosi was actually older than Silvesta Maweu. He was thirty-four, with two children from his six years of marriage. At one time, he had been Maweu's teacher for some months before he had resigned from teaching and started working with a community development organisation.

Simon Mosi and Swastika Nzivele walked down the road for a while just to make sure that no untoward impressions were left behind about them. Mosi pushed the BSA bicycle proudly, his face gleaming.

'Can you ride?' he asked her.

'A bicycle?'

'Yes.'

'Unfortunately, no. Father had a bicycle which was only for the boys, never for the daughters.'

'What do you think of bicycle riders?'

'What's there to think about them? Are they some kind of special people?'

'Not that.'

'What is it?'

'Their status I mean.'

'I've never thought about it.'

'You know what? I don't know whether it is the same in Kangundo, your place . . . I guess it is so everywhere . . . People here think that riding a bicycle is a sign of poverty. But if you live around here you soon discover that the best transport in the country is the bicycle, really. It's so cheap to maintain. It needs no petrol, no broad roads, no bridges; and when something goes wrong, you do not have to take it for repair all the way to Masaku or Nairobi. But, of course, it has its limitations. There is no roof over your head when you are riding a bicycle. I guess you and your husband would never dream of riding one.'

'Who told you that?'

'Me. The two of you are great idealists.'

'You must have a very bad impression of us, Simon.'

Simon Mosi helped her on to the bicycle as soon as they were out of sight from the shops. She gripped his waist with her hands. He made the first turn of the pedals feeling her comfortable body laid against his back. The bicycle zig-zagged at first, scaring her.

'Are you falling already?' she asked tightening her grip on him.

There was no need for an answer because the bicycle steadied and took a straight line. Nzivele's legs caught the fresh cool air, cooling her. The bicycle picked up speed and rolled down the slope fairly fast. For a moment, they didn't speak to each other. Nzivele's skirt flapped fiercely in the wind.

'Are you still there?' Simon Mosi asked her as if he didn't feel her.

'Very much,' she said with a soft laugh which he didn't hear but felt in the movement of her body.

'You know what, Nzivele?'

'Tell me.'

'I feel honoured to give you a lift . . . Thou art great, knowest thou?' he said in English.

'What am I?'

'Well, I thought you might be stand-offish . . . People of your standard of living don't usually go for these cheap means of transport. Actually, come to think of it, you must be a broad-minded person. Your attitude to life and teaching is required to civilise the people of this place.'

'What standard, Simon? You don't know what you are talking about.'

'You think I don't?'

'I have no standard, no civilisation. Maweu and I don't even have a motorbike, let alone a car. You are much better than we are because you have a bicycle. You can give us a lift, but we can't give you one!'

'A bicycle costs a few thousands of shillings only.'

'Which we don't have, you see.'

'Nonsense, your *ukutak utany'o*. You are trying to be modest.'

'What would your wife say if she heard that you had given me a lift?'

'She knows that I give people lifts – men and women. '

The bicycle hit a stone and went out of control for a while. Nzivele tightened her grip on him so hard that he could hardly breathe. She shut her eyes and clenched her teeth, ready to fall. But Simon Mosi managed to regain control.

'God!' she exclaimed.

'I'm sorry, Nzivele,' he apologised. 'But I can assure you that you are safe. These murram roads are terrible.'

The sun was beginning to set. The radiance of the sunset covered the hills, giving them such an awesome appearance that it seemed as if the biblical Moses might show up, walking on one of them. The air was dry and fresh, pleasantly warm.

'It's a gorgeous sunset,' he told her, feeling the pressure of her breasts against his back, an enjoyable feeling. She was comfortable, enjoying the experience, though it was frightening at times. She moulded herself to him expertly like someone who had often been given lifts on a bicycle without any stiffness, freely as if she wanted to donate her whole body to him. For some reason this reminded him of a Chinese poem written many hundreds of years earlier which he used to recite:

The mountain air is fresh at the dusk day

The flying birds two by two return.

In these things there lies

A deep meaning; yet

When we would express it

Words suddenly fail us.

Nzivele laid her head on his back, her right temple resting against his broad shoulder-blade. She had ended up buying a lot, nearly a basketful. Simon had the basket in front of him tied on the frame. He could do a lot with a bicycle, even carrying three persons on it.

'Do you know that I have been moved from Nunguni to work around Kitandi, so near my home? I'm very happy.'

'Permanently?' she asked in his ear. 'That's the word, thank God.'

'What a lucky man!'

'I think I am. Now I won't have to push the bicycle all the way up the hill. They have embarked on a project near Kitandi which includes some geological investigations.'

'It's so nice to work near home.'

'I agree.'

The road became rough and cut off their conversation. Mosi's shoulders vibrated above Nzivele's head, reacting to the shocks.

Mosi was a very hard-working man, in spite of his moods. He had fallen short of sitting for school certificate, unlike Nzivele and Maweu, but he had passed his junior secondary very well. Then he had been unable to raise the fees to continue with his education. After leaving school, he had developed a great interest in farming, which he did now, combining it with his community development job where he worked more or less as a clerk.

Nzivele had often admired his farm across the river - the way it was laid out, the evergreen pawpaw trees, the *kathuku* bananas, the orange and lemon trees, the mango trees, the avocado trees, the castor apples . . . When the season was good for the oranges and the lemons, you could pick out the trees yellow with ripe fruit from a long distance away. Sometimes Nzivele imagined she could see them from her house, although it was too far for such details to be visible. Everything in Simon's garden was artistically planned, in pretty lines and circles, on beautiful terraces which spanned the slope of the land in long arcs. His house, which had a green roof, lay hidden among large mango trees. His first job in agriculture, which he had had for a few years, had benefited him tremendously, for it was during this time that he had acquired the knowledge of farming. It was here where the white agricultural officer had told him, 'If you have a piece of land, you must plan its development as seriously as you would budget your money; and you should never, ever, leave a portion of that land idle.'

Mosi had taken those words very seriously. He had seven acres of land only, but he seemed to grow everything he wanted and needed. On the eastern part of his pretty garden, he had a hundred eucalyptus trees growing very tall.

'Does your wife like it now that you work near your home?' Nzivele asked. He was pushing the bicycle uphill after trying to ride up a little way, his bottom off the seat so that he could exert more force on the pedals while Nzivele sat behind him lazily, pulled ahead by every expensive turn of the pedals, watching Mosi's behind swing left and right; he was puffing. 'Good exercise,' he had said when getting off.

'My wife . . .' he said thoughtfully. 'Of course she's happy that I'm working around. Now I'll concentrate more on the farm. I've bought two more acres next to the farm, on Muthoka's side. He sold them to me to pay school fees for his children.'

Then Simon Mosi made the statement that changed Nzivele for the rest of her life. 'Some men, like your husband for example, are extremely lucky to marry a wife who is both beautiful and hard-working. I would have been a different man if such fortune had come my way – especially the hard-working bit.'

Nzivele didn't respond immediately. She sat silently, thinking about his words, and letting them sink, sink, and soak into her mind. He had touched her emotions unexpectedly, invading her privacy and forging a link between them.

'You really think I'm like that, Simon?' came a very soft voice, trying to hide her feelings. She sighed.

Mosi's house had a window facing Nzivele's house. The two mango trees didn't obstruct his view through the window. At night, when she wanted to call him, she took her lantern and went out at a particular time. Simon Mosi saw the light and knew everything was safe.

So he responded. But Makenzi always raised hell and attracted Kalunde's attention by his powerful and impatient barking when Mosi was coming, although he never bit Simon because he knew him. He barked a greeting, not a protest.

It would be accurate to say that Simon Mosi and Nzivele fell in love, or they began to sin, or misbehave, as people put it. For quite some time, the change in Nzivele confused or blinded Maweu. He thought that his wife must have settled down emotionally in that, if he failed these days to turn up from Mombasa even for a full month, when he did finally come home she didn't make the hell out of it that she had done at the beginning. She appeared less demanding, more understanding and tactful, choosing her words carefully and treating him to a nice welcome, prettily dressed.

When Maweu came home and heard that Makenzi had died, he asked Nzivele a direct question as if the spirit of Makenzi had told him the truth.

'Nzivele did you poison Makenzi?'

'What?' she cried leaping up as if he had struck her.

'Ah, take it easy,' he said embracing her. 'It was a joke – what do you think?' He thought he felt some sort of trembling in her body, but he ignored it.

Nzivele heaved a big sigh, disengaged herself from the embrace and walked out of the house, sweating. She stood outside, feeling the strong heartbeat in her breast, staring into the dark. There was no light in Mosi's house. She wondered whether the story of her trying to get the poison had leaked out to her husband in any way.

'I'm treading on dangerous ground,' she said to herself. But in that instance, the full features of Simon Mosi came back to her mind, then a voice from within her said, 'He who cannot die for love is not worthy of it.'

''Nzivele!' She heard the voice of her husband calling.

'Yes,' she said and heard the creaking of the door as he was coming out, following her.

'Come please, let's be friends.' He touched her shoulder. 'Don't stand in the cold.' He wound himself round her and kissed her neck, then led her back to the house.

'It was a stupid joke,' he told her.

'What a joke!' she thought.

7

◆ ◆ ◆ ◆

Someone must have tipped off Maweu that his wife was running wild and his mother was starving. He decided to carry out his own investigation by coming home at a time when nobody expected him. He had also discovered that his weak mother was trying to hide information from him. Earlier on, when he had demanded to know why she had lost so much weight and why her clothes looked so dirty, she had defended herself. 'Old age has many trials, son. I have always some pain here and there, and my appetite is not good.'

It was on a Wednesday at six when he arrived home on a three-day leave. He would be going back on Sunday. The Saturday gave him an additional day.

The winding path from the main road took him down and down to his home. He didn't want to think about anything just yet; during the next four days he would have enough time to find out everything he needed to know. He was expecting to find his wife at home but, instead, he found only a padlock hanging on the door. Worse still, he had forgotten his own key to the house when he had left Mombasa. The sight of the padlock infuriated him immediately. Everything he could see seemed to tell him that Nzivele had been away for a long time.

'Damn this!' he cursed, and threw his leather suitcase on the ground by the door. He walked over to his mother's house. It too was dead silent, without a single sign of life – not even a chicken anywhere. The compound was dreadfully neglected.

'What?' he said aloud finding that his mother, too, was not around. He thought for a moment. Possibly the two were just about to arrive. He was about to go to the neighbour's home to find out where his people had gone when he saw one of them – the wreck of his mother appearing about a hundred yards away. She was coming from the river, carrying a small gourd of water.

'Oho! So this is it!' he said aloud and felt a heat start from within as he watched, amazed, at the approaching figure of his mother. 'Has my wife gone away completely?' A wave of anger washed over him. He could not believe what he was seeing. His mother, who saw him as she drew nearer, didn't like the fact that he had seen her carrying a gourd of water. She didn't speak to him immediately; Maweu was also silent. He found himself searching, fumbling for the right word and trying to adjust his emotions to deal with the situation. For the first time, he didn't know what to say to his mother.

Without moving, he watched her until she disappeared into the house. Just before she got inside, he called her automatically, 'Mother!' but said nothing when she groaned an answer.

'I'm talking to you, Mother,' he said, standing by the door. 'Don't you hear my voice?'

After some silence the voice of his mother replied from the house, 'Why don't you come into the house first?'

'Where's Nzivele?'

'I must sit down first, please,' she said and brought a stool out from the house. She then groaned with backache as she lowered her body to sit. 'Won't you sit down?' she added. 'It's brighter here outside, take a stool.'

'Where's Nzivele?' he repeated, like a computer.

She groaned again and remained silent.

He didn't press her, she always took her time. Meanwhile, he went into the house and came out with a stool.

'I thought she was in her house,' Kalunde said finally, in as calm a voice as she could muster.

'Was there nobody who could have gone for the water?'

'Why?' she blew her nose to the side, then turned to greet him, '*Wakya* Maweu!'

'*Aa!*' he answered the greeting painfully.

'I don't know where Ng'aMbalu is.'

'Didn't you see her today?'

She kept silent. 'Has she run away?'

'No, she's still here.' It was a forced answer.

'Where? Dead?'

'Why do you boil so? Find her in her house.'

'The house with the padlock – is Nzivele dead?' he barked, unable to bear the riddles in his mother's answers.

'What a question!'

He rose to his feet angrily and started talking loudly, stammering. 'I want to know where she is . . . Then why you should be going to the river for water – number one, when there's money to employ people to do so, and, number two, when Nzivele could go for the water, if she has to.'

'I'm also waiting for her.'

'Also waiting?'

'What do you think?'

He snorted and scratched over his thighs. 'Why are your clothes so dirty, Mother? You look sick, dying!'

'That's right.'

'That's right what? What is going on here?'

'Of course I'm dying. You and I are not of the same age.' She changed the subject. 'How is it where you have come from?'

He ignored her question and walked away, round his house as if he expected to find Nzivele somewhere behind it. He returned to his mother.

'When did she go away?'

'You ask me?'

'Whom should I ask?'

Kalunde broke loose and talked like someone tired of everything, 'You come to ask me where your wife is . . . I never see that wife of yours these days. I only hear her opening and closing the door, or laughing with other people. She comes home and locks herself up in the house and that's everything, the story ends there. '

'When last did you eat, Mother?' He felt near to tears.

'Me? That's a silly question.'

'Do you eat?'

'Would I be living if I didn't eat?'

He shouted at her. 'Mother, when did Nzivele last give you food – talk straight!'

Kalunde didn't reply. She kept her eyes staring at the ground before her, holding herself still like a stump, and regretting that she had been so blunt. Perhaps, she thought, she could have said it in a more diplomatic way.

'Did she leave the key with you?'

'Would she?'

Maweu lost his temper. First he wandered about, then walked steadfastly to his house and kicked the door so violently that it tore off from its lower hinges and dangled forlornly. Another kick sent it flying inside. A brick fell off from the wall and hit his foot. He cursed and hit the wall hard. Kalunde didn't stir an inch; perhaps she was too tired to do anything, or it could have been that nothing really mattered to her any more. While dust still smoked from the house through the dark opening where the door had been, Maweu walked away without quite knowing where he was going. The sun had already gone down and the grey of the twilight had started blurring everything. He walked up the slope, but he turned and started walking down in the opposite direction. Then he changed course again and walked in yet another direction.

Maweu looked at his watch. Nine thirty at night. Yet Nzivele still hadn't come home. He felt the pain of it all, circulating in his bloodstream. He remembered with sadness the words of his friend, Wambua, 'There are certain wives who are too many tons to carry on your back.'

His mother stirred in her chair where she had been sitting in long spells of silence, sometimes staring at the weak light of the lantern. She would have loved to know what her son was thinking and what he was planning to do. She had told him everything: about the dances and Simon Mosi. He had listened to the humiliating story patiently, letting every word sink in. The weak voice of his mother said what she had never thought of revealing to her son.

'Really?' he said, staring at the smoky glass of the lantern. The dark, flat face of his mother stood in the dim light like a sculpture. A small fire burned between them on the deep hearth. Kalunde's bony legs covered in white nail-scratches showed up faintly. The atmosphere had been so bad that they hadn't even thought of eating. What would they eat anyway? Some hours earlier in the afternoon, she had tried to pound some cooked maize grains in the mortar to make herself some paste which she had sat down and tried to eat - but it had taken nearly one full hour. She had a painful loose tooth, but she didn't want to have it pulled out because it would mean even fewer teeth being left in her mouth.

The fire burned in Maweu's head. At that moment, he didn't know what course of action he would take when Nzivele finally returned. That is, he thought, if she was going to come at all that night.

'Simon Mosi . . . ' he spoke through his lips; then he began to think or wonder what he could do to him, or say, if they met face to face.

Kalunde gathered herself and rose to her feet, joints cracking. Without saying anything, she walked out of the house slowly, into the dark to ease herself. It might also have been her intuition at work, because just as she was coming back to enter the house, she heard a brief cry at Maweu's house. It was Nzivele reacting to the shock of finding her house without the door. Kalunde thought fast, very fast, and instantly changed her course. She ran in the direction from which the voice had sounded and nearly bumped against Nzivele who was running towards Kalunde's house. Kalunde hushed her and, hoping that Maweu hadn't heard the cry, she stammered, 'Ng'aMbalu . . . you are, please . . . you are dead if Maweu sees You.! Run away and find a place to sleep – my child, go away now!'

Faintly, Maweu must have heard the cry, but it took time for him to digest what was happening. He came out, but by the time he reached the house, he only heard the footsteps of Nzivele retreating beyond their house. Then there was a big thud – she must have stumbled and fallen down before springing to her feet again and fleeing in the moonlight.

'What was that, Mother?' he asked Kalunde when she re-turned. She didn't answer. Instead, she re-entered the house, wondering about the strange coincidence that she had gone out at the right moment. 'Thank God,' she said as she came in.

'Was that Nzivele?' her son croaked, feeling that his mother was trying to cover up something.

'Whom did you think it was?' Kalunde raised her voice.

'Where is she?'

'She ran away.'

'Why – for goodness sake, why?'

'Why? Maweu, aren't you stupid sometimes!' She spoke harshly. 'So you thought you could break the door, then have her to break too? I told her to run away. Beat me up instead, not Ng'aMbalu.'

There was silence during which Maweu tried to puzzle out what was happening. Was there some conspiracy between the two?

'You can go to bed now,' Kalunde said, after sitting down. She didn't want to talk any more.

Nzivele remained away for the whole of the next day. Maweu had gone in the morning to two places where he hoped to find her, in neighbours' homes, but she wasn't there. He didn't ask the neighbours whether she had been seen around.

Kalunde had actually woken up in the morning and gone to the only place she knew Nzivele could have run for refuge – the Mawias'. In normal cases, Nzivele wouldn't have gone to the pastor's home but, today, she had probably taken Kalunde's advice of happier days. She knew that, even if Maweu followed her there and lost his temper before the pastor, he couldn't beat her because he respected the pastor greatly. Since Nzivele had started running loose, she had been dodging the pastor. She couldn't stand his stare that seemed to carry God's power with it.

Nzivele knew very well her father's stand towards Maweu. If she dared run to her father's home to hide, and her father found out the truth about her, he would turn all his spikes against her. He knew that she was a difficult daughter, and he knew that Maweu was a decent son-in-law who, with his kind mother, would not be mean to his daughter.

At about ten o'clock when Maweu returned from his search for his wife, he found Pastor Joana Mawia talking to Kalunde outside her house. Maweu got a grip on himself and went to shake hands. They exchanged a few words, none of which touched on Nzivele. The pastor tried to ignore the conflict, and Maweu was not keen on bringing it up. He was simply worried about where she had gone, and he knew that his mother was not going to tell him anything.

Maweu started repairing the door of his house. The pastor came and gave him a helping hand, but he didn't ask Maweu what had happened to the door until two hours later, when the door was back in its place. .

'I kicked it off,' Maweu told the pastor.

Joana Mawia seemed to take it lightly. First, he gave a little laugh, then asked, 'Maweu, why would you break off your own door?'

'I was angry.'

'Ah, yes . . . They say that an angry man is a man riding a mad horse . . . ' He paused. 'But, you know, anger has destroyed more homes than it has made. If you had tried to contain it, you and I wouldn't have spent the whole morning repairing this door, would we? We would have been doing other things, better ones, perhaps.'

Maweu remained silent.

'Where's your wife?' the pastor asked at last.

'My wife?'

'Yes, your wife.'

Maweu replied with ease, 'I don't know. She wasn't here when I came yesterday – that was what the door was broken for . . .' He studied the pastor's eyes.

'And you mean she hasn't shown up since yesterday?'

Maweu nodded. 'Why?'

Maweu clicked his tongue and kept silent.

'Why, Maweu?'

'I think she came back and Mother scared her away . . . I don't have a wife. To be frank with you, I would have broken her neck last night if I had got hold of her.'

'Maweu, do you know what you are saying?'

'Even if I don't know, I have an idea. I'm telling you what I feel.

Pastor Mawia smiled, 'What you feel is not what is right always.'

'You know what that thing you call my wife did?'

'She is not a thing; she is your wife.'

'Whatever she is, do you know what she did?'

'Never mind, nothing she did could have deserved her neck being broken. You shouldn't say that, son.'

'I would have given her a beautiful beating,' he said, looking at his own hands.

'Thank God your mother scared her away.'

Maweu stared at the pastor. They were sitting in his house at the table, facing each other.

'The neck of a human being is too precious to be broken,' the pastor continued.

'You've no idea,' Maweu raised his voice. 'You don't know what the evil she is doing.'

'You are trying to blow up the issues,' came the calm reply, as if they were discussing unimportant things.

'Don't you see Mother, then hear the stories circulating around about that porcupine you call my wife?'

'I see your mother, yes. And, Nzivele is not a porcupine. I told you that she is your wife. Even when your child is a thief, he is still your child.'

'What reasoning is this?'

'Mature reasoning, Maweu. What you seem to forget is that adult life is not easy. Other people live with worse problems than yours.'

'*Ata we?*' Maweu became heated. 'When she is killing my own mother?'

'Maweu.' The pastor shut his eyes, then pressed his face with his hands, painfully. He took his time thinking. 'Maweu, I don't say that what your wife is doing is good.' He looked Maweu in the eye. 'I see your problem too . . . But, it is a problem that can be solved. Shall I tell you something?'

'Of course, do.'

'Yes.' He said and covered his face again as if saying a prayer. When he uncovered his face, he spoke again.

'Maweu, your success is measured by how many problems you have solved. And your bravery will be counted according to the number of problems, great problems, you solve.'

Maweu grunted.

'You should see this as a trial, as a challenge,' the pastor added, feeling about himself. His hands must have been looking for his dear Bible.

'Then what type of wife have I?'

'The type is not what matters, but what you can make of her. You will not believe it if I tell you that no wife is like another. The problem that made you kick off that door is a problem that another man would face calmly.'

'Why are you trying to make it sound so easy?'

'Ah, you are the one trying to make it sound so grave!'

'You mean I'm crazy, Pastor?'

'You are just inexperienced . . . You are quite young. Many things are on their way to you. Your wife has a small problem perhaps, which you surprisingly don't understand.'

'For Christ's sake what problem?' Maweu hit the table with his fist.

'Let's spare the table.' The pastor spoke jokingly.

Maweu continued, 'I send this bloody . . .'

'Son, don't use that language,' the pastor interrupted him. 'We are talking about your wife.'

'Do I not send her all the money she needs and, besides that, am I not here every other weekend?'

'If she had no problem, she wouldn't do what she does.'

'I thought your entire mission was to preach against sin!'

'You are right.'

'What about it now?'

'The word of the Lord says everything about man. There are many who are in the lead now, who will come last in the end. Maweu, sin has its own force. And, often, for you to banish sin, you may have first to be given love and tolerance. The life of a woman has many temptations. God Himself knows that. My own father used to tell me that a woman is a delicate load which needs great care in handling. The truth is not far from that . . . '

'You are asking me to nod at what is happening, and let this woman feed me with dirt?

'No, that's not so.'

'Then what are you telling me?'

'To receive your wife as your load, give her guidance where she needs it and find out what problem she has. That's how to be a responsible husband; you don't become one by breaking her neck. Do you see that?'

'You want to confuse me, Pastor.'

'I would be making a big mistake, also committing a big sin, Silvesta. Your wound is my wound. It is true that you have been giving your wife all the money she needed, but money is not the answer to everything. There are a lot of people who have all the money they need on earth, yet they commit great crimes and sins. You should handle this problem calmly. It's a big problem, we all know that, but you must practise sound judgment and tolerance – those two are the greatest pillars to any life.'

'I still don't understand fully what you are advising me to do really.'

The pastor brought his head forward and closer like someone who wanted to tell a secret. 'Maweu life is very difficult . . . Without faith in both yourself and the Lord, and without a good heart for people, you can't live a steady life. What your wife is today, and what she has done, does not say or imply what she will be in the future. Sooner or later, you and Nzivele are going to be parents . . . As parents, both of you will learn that when your child falls sick, it will be your sole responsibility to have the child treated. And I can assure you that, at that time, never once in the course of your child's illness, will you say that you have had enough trouble with the child and, therefore, you should abandon him and let the illness kill him . . .' He paused and held his hands together into one fist. 'Do you think that's true?'

Maweu nodded, 'I think it is . . . '

'Thank you,' the pastor said, raising his index finger. 'If you know what I am saying, then you should see that Nzivele is your child. To abandon her is one thing which you should never think of, or to break her neck. She is a sick child, and your sole responsibility is to treat her.'

'Has she been treating my mother?'

'How could she? A sick person does not treat another. Sickness is of many kinds . . . Your wife is too young to know what she is doing … She needs an understanding and patient hand!'

'If she loves Simon Mosi like that, why shouldn't she marry him and remove this bitchy behaviour from my home?'

'You shouldn't rush into conclusions.'

'You can't feel it because it is not your problem.'

'That's an easy statement, Silvesta. By the time you have reached my age, you will say different things. Life is never what it was yesterday . . . Simply, we are never the same people we were yesterday.'

'You really think I should listen to . . . ' He hit the table, sighed and stood up.

The pastor's eyes rested keenly on him.

8

◆ ◆ ◆ ◆

Only after Silvesta Maweu had vowed to Kalunde that he would not fight Nzivele, did Kalunde send for her. It was the afternoon when she returned. Maweu was lying on his bed, his thoughts going in circles. Kalunde was sitting outside her house, eating from the memory of her past life. The figure of Nzivele found her way to the house, her face full of uncertainty and terror. She came and stood near Kalunde and said nothing, then started biting her nails, waiting for Kalunde to say something.

'*Wakya Ng'aMbalu?*' Kalunde greeted her. '*Aa!*' she answered shyly.

Kalunde made a sign with her chin that Maweu was in the house and Nzivele should go in. The girl took a few steps and then stood outside the house, feeling the race of her heart. The pastor's wife had treated her very well and hadn't gone into details regarding the cause of the conflict.

Nzivele looked at the door and studied the repairs. She wanted to go in, but she lacked the courage, suspecting that Maweu would pounce on her and, in his own words, give her a good beating.

'How shall I get in?' She sighed worriedly. 'I guess I've just got to do it.' With that thought, she turned the handle of the door, but it seemed locked. No, she hadn't tried it properly. Her second attempt released the door and she made her way in nervously, holding her breath, teeth clenched. She closed the door behind her, then thought she shouldn't have closed it. She opened and left it free, just in case her husband decided to attack her . . . she could escape easily.

She stood in the centre of the living room. On the long sofa was a book with its pages open in the middle lying face downwards. She looked at the title. *The Concubine*.

'Concubine?' In spite of her fear she grinned.

Maweu made a coughing noise and that sent lightning cutting through her stomach. Her every limb felt weak. She stirred up and held her breath, sweating, wondering what she should tell him. Perhaps, she thought, the best thing was to keep silent, not to try to answer any of his provocative questions. She was hungry for she had hardly eaten for worrying.

'Why do I do these things?' she blamed herself. Something strong, perhaps the force that the pastor had been talking about, had pushed her into all this, into doing what she already knew was wrong, and was bound to hit back at her. 'I think I'm becoming weak and silly,' she thought. Yet, she couldn't dismiss things as simply as that. She believed in the words of her father, that theory is different from actual life. She realised that there are many things in life that people do, for example, even when they know that those things are harmful to themselves, yet they can't help doing . . . Kalunde's action had taken Nzivele by surprise, and she had begun wondering whether, after all, Kalunde approved of her.

She was still standing there, fighting within herself on what to do when she caught sight of the figure of her husband appearing at the bedroom door. She started, gasped and said nothing, avoiding his eyes though she wanted to see all his movements. Maweu stood there for a long time, staring at her. And she stood, waiting for whatever was destined to come. Her feet felt light, ready to carry her away instantly if the worst struck. He was really punishing her by holding her in that suspense. She wished he would say something, not stand there still staring at her, his left leg crossed over his right, hanging his left hand by the thumb over the pocket of his trousers, his other arm akimbo, and his trunk leaning on the door frame.

He also wanted to say something to her, but that something didn't come . . . It was there in the mouth, but the tongue was too heavy.

'Well . . . ' He sent a streak of fright through her. 'Did you come here to stand or to sit?'

She sat down urgently, without saying anything, then rubbed her nose, looking away though keeping his figure in sight at the corner of her eye.

'Where have you come from?' he asked calmly.

She stirred up, but produced no single word, then began to wring her fingers and crack her knuckles.

'I think you must speak!' He walked from the door and took a seat opposite her.

'Where have you come from?'

'Pastor's.' She held herself like a schoolgirl.

'What were you doing there?'   .

'Well,' she sighed, and kept quiet for a while. 'Mother asked me to go there.'

'Because that's your 'home?'

'No.'

'Why did she ask you to go there?'

Nzivele only sighed.

'What's up with you?' he barked.

She started.

'Why did you run away last night?'

'I was afraid you'd beat me.'

'Why did you think I'd do that?'

'I mean . . .' She began to cry into her hands. He watched her, unmoved by her tears, wondering why she was crying. Was she crying because she was sorry for what she had done, or merely because she was afraid that he would beat her?

That time, nothing spectacular happened between Nzivele and Maweu – no drama, that is. Maweu returned to Mombasa. Nzivele had shown every sign that she was gravely sorry for her conduct. The two didn't talk much though.

Pastor Joana Mawia had defused Maweu's anger, or rather, postponed it. Maweu left his mother unhappily, mainly because she wasn't feeling well. She complained of an acute pain in her left rib cage. She looked weak, and he worried that she might not live until his return two weeks hence.

The next night, Kalunde had her nightmare again. But this time, the dream had a strange ending: she tried to climb out of the lake, two or three times falling back into the water, still screaming for help. Meanwhile, she saw Maweu standing somewhere far off, looking to the east, away from Kalunde's direction. He stood on raised ground. The sun was shining into his face. This time, Kalunde managed to climb out of the water and walked up. But she found herself standing very high on an embarkment that had the lake on one side, and a great waterfall on the other side. She became terrified that she would fall over. But something happened and she found herself now at the bottom of the waterfall, standing a little way from the place the water poured. She looked up at the waterfall. On the embarkment where she had been standing, she saw Maweu and his wife playing about dangerously, in a way that they meant they were in danger of falling over. The water came down in a big deluge, pounded the ground and splashed up high again. Kalunde was terrified that Maweu and his wife would fall over and crash down with the water. She also feared that she would get lost. But then, the scene changed. She saw big bubbles forming at the base of the waterfall. When these bubbles exploded, they hatched out children who ran down the stream in big numbers, then started flying away like birds. Small children, with a red mark round their neck, with feet which were rather thin like bird's.

For about three months, Nzivele returned to her yoke, taking care of Kalunde, although not with the old enthusiasm. She tried to dodge Simon Mosi successfully, or at least, convinced her conscience that it was a very bad thing that she was doing. Kalunde became much better and started enjoying the renewed good relationship with her daughter-in-law.

But then, this feeling she had about Simon Mosi began to return, agonisingly . . . especially on one particular night . . . It was pouring cats and dogs. The rain hit the iron sheet roof as if it would destroy the house, which was beaten even more violently by a strong wind. This was the two-bedroomed house that Maweu had built, which he intended to turn into a kitchen when his big house was finished. But the idea of the big house had been forgotten since Nzivele started running wild. They had continued to live in this small one, over-crowded with furniture.

She was lying on her back, her eyes staring helplessly and blankly at the dark. When the lightning struck, she saw the rafters of the roof. She was scared rigid by the storm. It was long past midnight, but she hadn't slept a wink. The major thing was that Simon Mosi had come to her mind strongly tonight. She thought about him in circles, worrying that, as she now felt so weak, the whole affair was going to come to life again. It was the feeling that an alcoholic who has stopped drinking for a full year has, then finds himself tempted back by a bottle he is fondling in his hands . . . She could blame herself as much as she wanted for the attachment, and people could condemn her in whatever way they wanted, but the force behind her was another thing altogether. She loved Maweu all right, no question about that, but then Silvesta Maweu was not Simon Mosi. There was something else deep inside Simon Mosi which she couldn't explain. Something that made her so vulnerable to him – a great delicacy in Mosi.

Perhaps it wouldn't have started all over again if she hadn't met him the previous afternoon. He must have known that she had gone to Koola Town. There was only one way she could take coming home. So, Simon Mosi had gone to waylay her. Nzivele was coming back from Koola Town with other women when she caught sight of the figure of her lover ahead of them, walking in the same direction, slowly. She knew what he intended immediately. He must have seen her coming and started walking, just to confuse the other two women.

'Who's that now?' she thought, cutting off what she had been saying to the other women. She recognised him very well from his back view. Her feelings churned inside her. She felt weak, and was hit by an urge to ease herself.

'Hold this basket for me, please,' she told one of her companions. 'I'm pressed, and must branch off for a while.' Or maybe she wanted to have some time to think about how to behave when she met this Simon Mosi.

'Nzivele, please,' her companion answered, 'we have a long way to go, and the weather is not good. Why don't you let us run, please. You see those heavy clouds? Take the basket with you – you are nearly at home.'

They were not actually trying to excuse themselves because they had seen Simon Mosi in front of them. None of them could have recognised him from the back anyway, except Nzivele. She took the basket, but stood there for a while, digesting what the companions meant. However, it would make it easier for her to meet Simon Mosi. She would still be forced to stop to shake hands with him, even if she stayed in their company.

When she returned to the path, she saw Simon Mosi standing about three hundred yards from her. She walked to him, nervously, with a blank mind, her feet just carrying her along. She hadn't seen him for two months, at least; mainly because he had been away. More than three months before, she had met him and told him that she wouldn't be able to continue with this agonising attachment.

'I don't blame you for that,' he had told her.

'So?'

'Wait until I'm dead, then you can say that . . . ' Nzivele seemed to be aware of every part of her body, as she walked to the man, waiting . . . The evening sun was full on her face when the big cloud had passed by.

She stood before him, then waited. A kind of pain showed in his face. He shook hands with her, but could not say a word for some time. Each took some uncertain steps forward, and it took a long time before they started talking. Then he persuaded her to move from the path. 'Let's find a place where passing people cannot see us . . . just to have two or three words together, please.'

It was around five. It wasn't going to be long before it started pouring. Already, the Mbooni hill was half covered by dark rain. However, it would be at least an hour before the rain arrived where they stood.

'Did you come just to meet me?' she asked when they were seated.

'What a question!'

She wanted to say something to put him off, but only the nice things found their way out of her mouth. Within no time at all, she was lost inside the forest of her emotion. Or rather, Simon Mosi's power paralysed her.

'Why do you actually . . . really, Simon, why do you come to me?' she asked, disturbed. They had been talking in circles, so far, saying nothing substantial.

'I thought you had asked me that question before.'

'Maybe I should ask you the same question again.'

'Well,' he licked his lips, 'there's something I find in you which I don't find in my wife – let me be very blunt with you.'

'What thing?' She tried to look serious.

'I don't know.'

'Then if you don't know what it is, it doesn't exist.'

'You're free to take it the way you want, Nzivele. It's my heart that feels this, not yours.'

'Maybe you've never tried to look for it in your wife – not seriously.'

'I have known her for many years, and we have been married for quite some time. I haven't found it yet. Then, again, I have told you, my wife takes me for granted . . . There's a lot of personal things we could discuss together, if you were that much interested, but . . . Well, maybe I should put it this way: I'm not looking for a replacement. She's still my wife . . . and probably, I would have continued living with her the way I had been if I hadn't met you.'

'What about my marriage? Do you want to wreck that?'

'That's a simple way of putting it, Nzivele. Are you not wrecking mine too?'

'You are blinding me.'

'Are you not doing the same thing to me?'

The parting was very difficult that evening. Then the agony returned . . . She arrived home around eight. So it was this meeting that had kept her awake until midnight. She would love this affair to come to an end, but she didn't know how to make that happen. Perhaps 'if she went to live with her husband in Mombasa, all this would die a natural death. But then, there was this old mother to take care of. Nzivele could see every reason why she should live here, but . . . For the few years that she had been married, if she had to be frank with herself, she had caught herself wishing that Kalunde's life would close, then she could go to live with her husband in Mombasa. If Kalunde had been another Makenzi, Nzivele wouldn't have minded going for another poison. But, poisoning a human being, she felt, was a different story. As it was, people said that she had perhaps neglected Kalunde like that in order to hasten the old woman's death.

Misfortune returned to Kalunde with more force. It seemed as if it was Simon Mosi who brought her this misfortune. Nzivele turned her heart against Kalunde as soon as Simon Mosi returned to the scene. Kalunde wished that something could strike her dead. If she had had any strength to climb up a tree, put a rope round her neck and hang herself, that was what she would have done. The soul in her looked for a way out, beating her inside from every point, yet found no exit. Day and night, she waited for her death, but it didn't come. She had already given up hope that Maweu would ever restore things to normal. She was back again to making her own meals, going to haul her own water if she had the energy to go down the river; otherwise, she did without water for a long time. Pastor Joana Mawia came to see her more frequently, bringing her food too once in a while, or sending a child over to her with some cooked food.

Nzivele had again started coming home late in the night. She felt ashamed that she hadn't lived up to her promise of changing and becoming a better person, and one of the ways of avoiding this guilt was to come back home during the night when Kalunde was not likely to meet her. Or perhaps, after all, Nzivele had resigned herself to the thought, 'Who cares? Let what may come, come.'

This time, Swastika Nzivele was worse than before. It looked as if now, really, she didn't care a damn. Meanwhile, her husband's work had become more pressing. He had been promoted and was required to work harder, with longer overtime hours than before. So he could only afford to come home once every month, or instead, Nzivele went down to visit him. The affair between her and Simon Mosi climaxed one day when the two disappeared for three days together. Nobody knew where they had gone.

Nzivele should have learnt a lesson from her husband's violence when he had broken the door that time. This time when he came back and heard what was being said about her in the village, and that Simon Mosi had his best grip on her yet, he turned his anger against her. This time, Kalunde could not have helped Nzivele. In any case, Kalunde was in her own house and couldn't be there to help her. When Maweu came, he didn't show his anger immediately. He spent the whole day meeting people, trying to find out as much as he could about his wife's obsession.

That night, he waited until he was sure that every body had gone to bed, or was asleep. It must have been after one o'clock. Until then, he had tried to keep himself busy with one thing or another, first with his mother, discussing general things. Nzivele went to bed at eleven and left him scribbling down things, arranging and rearranging the furniture. She thought he was restless or in a bad mood and should be left alone.

He checked on the door. It was securely bolted. Then he walked rather uncertainly to the bedroom with the lantern in his hand. Nzivele was fast asleep under the yellow blanket. Her peaceful sleep seemed to provoke him; he thought she was having a wonderful time, living on his sweat, neglecting his mother, and running with other men.

'I say,' he urged, shaking her by the shoulder. 'Wake up, I must talk to you.'

'Eh?' Her eyes flew open and she shielded them from the bright light. 'Talk to me?

'Yes.'

'What about, at this time of the night?'

He placed the lantern on the table and sat away from her. She turned and lay on her back.

'Sit up!' he said in a voice that she couldn't mistake for friendliness. She sat up in the end and waited.

In a rather formal voice, he began. 'I want you to tell me what is going on.'

'Where?'

'In my home.'

'Oh!' she sighed. Her nerves warned her that she was bound for a rough time. Better be polite, she thought.

'Did you hear my question?'

'I don't understand . . .' she said and swallowed.

'What have you made out of me, Nzivele?'

'But,' she produced a silly smile. 'Silvesta, what could I make out of you? I don't know what you are really thinking.'

Maweu repeated the question.

'Why? I haven't made anything out of you.'

'I will give you a choice: to decide between Simon Mosi and Silvesta Maweu.'

'Am I in Mosi's home?'

'But you sleep with him, don't you?' he thundered. She went dead silent.

'Do you?' He shot to his feet.

She wondered how she could answer such a tricky question. She knew it was pointless to say no; yet it would be very dangerous to answer yes.

'What question is this?' she asked in a shaken voice.

'Don't try to be foolish. You know what type of question it is and why I am asking it.' His voice had fallen a bit.

She remained silent.

'I'll make you talk!' He grabbed her by the hand and smacked her violently on the side. The smack she hadn't expected cracked loud enough for Kalunde to hear.

She screamed.

Then he couldn't stop fighting her. She rolled from the bed, came up, and fought her way to the living room, but Maweu was on her. Both burst into the living room, breaking furniture, as she pleaded with him to spare her. In that instant, a loud banging came on the door from outside and in between Nzivele's screams, Maweu heard the voice of his mother, calling.

'Come and fight your own mother, devil!' Kalunde cursed. She must have been using a heavy object to bang on the door. But Maweu didn't stop. He followed Nzivele in a fury, beating and cursing her. Nzivele heard Kalunde banging the door and calling and she heightened her appeal, calling Kalunde for help, struggling to reach for the main door. Maweu found her stronger than he had ever imagined. Then came one heavy bang on the door that didn't seem to have come from Kalunde, although it did.

'What a big fool do I have for a son!' Kalunde cried.

'Will you eat her if you kill her?'

Maweu stopped the fight, unbolted the door, let Kalunde in, then he walked out as soon as she had come in. He snarled, 'If I find that prostitute there from tomorrow onwards, I'll kill her!' He walked away into the night, Nzivele's crying getting fainter and fainter the farther he went from the house. Then, suddenly, she stopped crying.

Silvesta Maweu didn't come back home until the next day. He didn't find his wife there.

10

◆ ◆ ◆ ◆

She didn't come back even after the three more days that Maweu was around. During this time, Maweu and Kalunde had disagreed completely. She would not set her eyes on him, blaming him for the violence. 'What did you expect me to do, Mother?' he asked, feeling tearful.

'Wait until I'm dead, then you can kill her.'

'Was I killing her?'

'What were you doing, oiling her skin?'

'You are an extremely trying person, Mother.'

'You have beaten her, eh? What did you achieve?'

'I didn't want to do . . .'

She interrupted him. 'Are you going to give up your work to come to take care of me – are you?'

'I'll engage someone else to do all that for you.'

'Then make that person your wife?'

'What nonsense you are preaching to me, Mother!'

'There are many women all over Kilungu and elsewhere. This Nzivele of yours with bat ears is not the only woman. She should disappear from my life.'

'Ah! There were many other women you talked about before you married this one, don't forget.'

'I think you're too old to reason out things.'

'I am, eh? Your mother!' She was furious, burning him with her grey eyes.

'Well, then why do you talk blindly like this?'

'Go and tell that to the Kaiti River, not me.'

Silence held him for a while, then he spoke softly as if addressing himself. 'How on earth does one have control over someone like this devil you call Nzivele?'

'So I'm expected to keep on barking at her all the time, doing everything to make her life smooth, without ever teaching her physically that she is breaking my back? What is she? Of what use is a woman like that to me, really?'

'She is your wife,' Kalunde said, and walked back to her house.

'My what?' he asked. 'I'm ready to look for another wife, a real wife.'

Silvesta Maweu had been so disappointed by Nzivele that he didn't even bothered to go and check whether or not she had gone to her father's home. He made a temporary arrangement with a village woman to take care of Kalunde for two weeks until he returned home again. That was at the end of the month when he had money to make permanent arrangements. He planned to take one week off duty.

He had decided to kick Nzivele out of his life, but he didn't feel easy with himself while travelling to Mombasa. The two hundred and forty miles to cover by road, riding a slow bus, gave him enough time to think over everything. It was a very unfortunate thing, he felt, in spite of all, that he still loved this Nzivele. She stuck inside him, somewhere, and it was very difficult to knock her out. For the last few days, he had made every resolution that his future with this loose woman was no more. But it is one thing to make vows and resolutions, but a different thing to act on them. He, too, discovered that he had a great weakness for her. In spite of everything, she meant many things to him.

'I'm sure I'll get over it,' he said to himself. Of course, he was right, time has the facility for restoring everything, or destroying everything. However, as his friend Wambua had told him, we belong to the future, not the past; we live by the good things, not by the bad ones . . . Isn't it better to look on the good side of life, that you may have something good to live for . . . ? First, Maweu had been thinking that after six months or so, a year or two, he would have forgotten all about that 'swine' as he called her now, but today, after a few days, the thought of her was returning to his mind so force-fully that he could not ignore it.

'Go for her and forget all that,' his friend, Wambua, advised him over lunch the next day.

'You think I should keep on crying for a woman who gives her love to another man?' His eyes looked out at the ocean.

'I understand you, brother.'

'So?'

'That's what life is, you know . . . Getting another wom-an doesn't guarantee you she too wouldn't give her love to another man. It's always a gamble.'

Maweu thought over those words seriously. This morning, the longing to forget Nzivele had returned. But Wambua, like Kalunde, like Pastor Joana Mawia, seemed to treat it like a petty problem. Why? Maybe they were all right and he was wrong. Or maybe, it's the wearer who knows where the shoe pinches; he, Silvesta Maweu, was the one in the right.

'You know,' Wambua said. 'I had the same problem one time with my wife.' He had actually never spoken about it before; but now he felt compelled to mention it, partly because he liked Nzivele and didn't want Maweu to divorce her. Everybody seemed to have a liking for her.

'What did you do, then?' Maweu was curious. You don't feel lonely as soon as you discover that many people are like you and have gone through the same experiences.

'I decided to keep the wife and forget the nonsense. After all, it's the person who matters.'

'He who doesn't travel thinks . . .' Maweu was saying.

Wambua finished the sentence, '. . . thinks that his mother is the best cook.'

'That's it. I may be thinking that this Nzivele is the best woman on earth whereas, actually, there are better ones.'

'The forest is still very big,' Wambua finished, leaving Maweu with the words to think over.

By the evening, Maweu had decided that perhaps he should start looking round for another girl . . . Not that he had stopped loving Nzivele but, somehow, another woman might give better reasons either to love or to stop loving her. Sometimes, the answer is not from within, but from outside.

Silvesta Maweu didn't return to Kyandumbi as soon as he had expected. His employer had pushed his leave farther ahead. It was five weeks before he could come back.

He sent someone with money for his mother and asked the woman he had engaged to stay on until he came.

Exactly four weeks after Swastika Nzivele had disappeared, Silvesta Maweu got a long letter from her. Information had already reached him that she was, living with her parents.

Dear Silvesta,

I don't know whether I should write this letter to you or not. I am eaten up by the guilt of what happened between you and I. I do think that the situation is bad enough to kill what we once thought we needed . . . I have a problem in writing this letter, because I don't know where to start, whether I am doing the right thing, or what. But I think it is good sometimes to open your mouth and let out whatever wants to come out, even if it would be a sneeze or a cry – it may save a situation.

I guess that all about you and I is finished. But the main reason is because you wanted it finished. You said that if you found me at your house the next day, you would kill me. Following the experience of the fight, I thought I should take your words seriously. You will agree with me that you didn't give me any opportunity to say sorry to you. On the other hand, I thought that even to say sorry to you would change nothing at all.

I heard the questions you asked me before the beating. But I didn't think you wanted any answers. You were very convinced that I love Simon Mosi. The aim of this letter is not, however, to tell you whether or not I love him; but just, first of all, to tell you that

I feel I must apologise to you. You don't have to accept my apology. But I thought you deserved it. I know that it is all my fault, and I knew that you would react to it one day.

You and I have lived for some time . . . in love, let's say, but in quarrels too. But when everything has been said, it is good to be grateful for the good part of our relationship. You may think that I don't know how much you loved me; but I can assure you that I knew it very well. All I can say is that you are a nice man, and a very loving one. It is pointless for me to tell you that I loved you, and that I still do so, simply because you will not understand. Or, you may understand, but you may not have the heart to appreciate. Love that has been tried, my father says, develops many doubts.

Silvesta, you may not believe it, but what has been happening to me has never really been my intention. I think I just found my-self very lonely, or afraid of myself, and I just got involved. Country life has many problems - it's a whole barren world in which you find yourself in no other company but that of village and poorly educated women. I am not trying to argue that I am better than they are; but it is that they and I belong to different worlds. You will probably think that I am talking a lot of nonsense.

I think I have one great problem, call it a weakness. I can't exist like that without doing anything. That is, I feel that I must engage myself or be occupied by something concrete. Not just trying to supervise some labourers digging coffee holes or making terraces. I need something more than that.

After your day's work in Mombasa, you can stroll around, doing some window-shopping or sight-seeing, or go for a swim or to watch the sea as I know you like doing, or watch a movie. But what do I have in Kyandumbi or at Koola Town? I am sure I am not the only person seeing it that way. Until there are facilities in a place like that, you can expect worse things from younger people.

In the old days, people were kept busy by their social activities - dances, communal celebrations for circumcisions and childbirths, initiations, participation in clan affairs, looking after the livestock and large families, and so on. What have we today in that place? Nothing, absolutely nothing.

And yet, one is expected to live there happily. It is a nice place, but it lacks other things. The desert looks very beautiful, with all those sand dunes, and so on, as you might have seen in films; but no one would like to live in it, because it lacks other factors that are essential to life. Of course, I am not trying to liken Koola to the desert, but I am sure you know what I am trying to say. The place doesn't lack water alone, but many other things. I would love to live in a place like that, in the country, if there were other things to occupy my mind.

I don't know whether you can connect this with my behaviour. Had I been a teacher or something, maybe my time there would have been less boring. I didn't love that Mosi the way you thought. It was a problem deeper than that, and I have great doubt whether you will ever understand it. I am not trying to justify my behaviour. It goes without question that it was immoral . . . That was also the cause for my disagreement with your mother. It would be good for me to simply say that I got messed up . . . A friend of mine once told me that even paradise would be boring without some form of occupation.

I know your predicament: the problem with your mother who must be taken care of. But she, too, didn't understand it anyway. Her world and mine are different. She and I had many misunderstandings. But, above all, she had her own expensive demands.

I don't know what you will make out of this. I have tried to touch on the reason for my problems. As I write this, you might have already met another girl who promises to do better than me when you get married . . . But, I am sure, in one way or the other, all women are basically the same; and they have common problems.

My father has been terribly nasty to me. Mother, too, just like you. Nobody is ready to understand me. But, I have come home, the only place I should come to when the outside world has rejected me. I don't know what to promise you. I will stay around for some time, trying to gather my thoughts together and deciding what to do with myself. Maybe I should go to the city and try my luck at getting some sort of job.

Yours in love,

SWASTIKA NZIVELE

Silvesta Maweu finished the letter. He left it on the desk, walked around, then went upstairs in the bank to walk around, thinking or trying to digest the contents. It was the kind of letter he had never expected from Nzivele.

'Very thoughtful,' he nodded to himself, though feeling hurt that she had mentioned anything about Simon Mosi, although what she had said wasn't too bad . . . He returned to his seat, opposite his friend Wambua, who had been watching his changing face while he read the letter, occasionally wincing with pain. He thought of her statement – that she didn't know what to promise him.

What did she mean by that? His eyes met Wambua's.

'The swine has written this!' He waved the long letter at Wambua.

'How can your wife be a swine?' Wambua asked, signing papers. 'She writes at length, eh? You must have a whole mansion in her heart.'

Maweu produced a laugh.

'I saw your face,' Wambua added.

'What did you see in it?'

'It was all screwed up,' he said. His head came up then, seriously, he asked, 'Is she all right?'

'Yes,' Maweu answered, after a pause.

'Gone with the wind?'

Not yet, still with her father – that's what she tells me.'

'When is she coming back?'

'Pardon?' Maweu's mind had wandered.

'Let's go for her next weekend,' Wambua suggested. He had a car and that would make things easy.

'Aha!' Maweu swung his head, then sat up. He dropped a heavy sigh, then started feeling the letter with his fingers.

'Someone is going to take her from you, man.'

'It'd solve the problem.'

'You think so?'

'Wait a minute.' Maweu buried his face in his palms and stayed there, still, as if he was saying a prayer.

'No!' he broke out in the end, and shot to his feet.

'Meaning?' Wambua asked, staring at him, biting the bottom of his pen uncomprehendingly.

11

♦ ♦ ♦ ♦

The cold Mwanyani air bathed his face as his thoughts sought the answer to his problem by drawing inspiration from the passing scenes. Dry, beautiful air, carrying the living smell of countryside. The bus groaned its way up the Iveti hill from Machakos, on its way to Kangundo. It was late morning. Silvesta Maweu caught his breath at the sight of Machakos Town, down below, and the generous open view beyond. His eyes looked for Kilimanjaro in that direction, but the giant mountain had blotted itself out with clouds. Maweu had always liked this grand view, down into the Athi Plain, especially the view from the nearby Mua Hills. He sat by the window, on the left of the bus; he never liked sitting on the right hand of any vehicle.

Today, the travellers were unusually quiet, like people going for a burial, or for a *kithitu* ceremony. The bus was very full. Occasionally, the silence would be broken by someone coughing, or a child crying. The gears of this fairly old bus called *Wenda*, changed loudly, jerking the whole vehicle. Since morning, Maweu had been thinking about what he was going to tell Nzivele, worse still, her parents. He had decided, after all, to go to see her.

Well, he thought . . . Maybe when his eyes met hers, the right words would come. It often happens . . .

The tarmac finished and the bus started on the murram road, casting heavy dust behind it. Everybody's flesh trembled with the roughness of the road and, as if they had woken up, many people started talking, coughing, blowing their noses; others began laughing, and a few of those who took snuff – old men and women – took it. Maweu kept his eyes on the Kangundo hills - hills that reminded him always of Swastika Nzivele. Even the name, Kangundo, would never sound in his ears without bringing Nzivele into his memory.

'I think I should tell her parents the truth,' he said to himself. He could bet that Nzivele hadn't told them the cause of their fight.

Thirty minutes later, he was walking towards Nzivele's home. The banana leaves whispered and fluttered from both sides of the path, through the coffee plantation. Today, he didn't carry anything with him, as on other days, when he would always come carrying a basket with several kilos of sugar, tea leaves, some Kimbo or Cowboy cooking fat, and so on, for his in-laws. Nzivele's father loved drinking tea and anyone who brought home a stock of tea was a great person. But Maweu was not sure how these people would receive him today after he had fought their daughter. If he brought anything with him, he might be forced to return with it.

He plunged his hands into his pockets, slowed down his walking, and engaged in a weak whistling as soon as he was near the home. His heart started beating fast, expecting to meet Nzivele's face first. The path leading to the home was tidy, with a green, well-kept fence. The home was set amongst bananas and under two tall trees that Mbalu had planted when he was a schoolboy, On the right hand side grew a thick vine of passion-fruit, attached to a *kithulu* tree. The leaves of cassava plants, looking like fingers, danced a crazy dance to the wind among the plants. There was a smell of heat and ferment in the air. A goat bleated from somewhere behind the building as if to announce Maweu's arrival. The front of the main house came into sight. Round the wall of the house, ran a green skirting two-and-a-half feet from the ground. Last time Maweu had been here, the skirting had been brown. The house must have been repainted.

'I see only a padlock,' Maweu said to himself, looking at the door. He came to the compound and looked round. There was nobody there. The compound held three buildings - the family house, the son's house, very small, and a wooden barn.

Maweu walked round the house to check whether anyone could be sitting there. But there was nobody. He stood there for a while, puzzled. It was getting hot: it was a few minutes to noon. He walked over and stood under the *kithulu's* shade, thinking. Would the neighbours know where this family had gone? He thought of going to find out. But just before he started, he saw his mother-in-law coming, carrying a drum of water. He sighed, and remained where he was, still, like a stump. Perhaps she would not see him immediately. But as soon as she came to the middle of the compound, she looked all round as though she could smell him somewhere. Her eyes caught sight of him. She didn't resemble Nzivele much. It was the father whose eyes Maweu feared. But he felt much more at home with Nzivele's mother, Fibi Mathembo.

'*Ai, Muthonua!*' Mathembo exclaimed to her son-in law and greeted him, after which she unloaded the drum. He was happy that she was the first person he should meet.

'Somebody told me you had been seen coming, just now, so I hurried here. Nzivele's father is working in the garden.' She disappeared into the house, then popped her head out. 'Why don't you come in?'

'It's better outside here,' he replied, pocketing and un-pocketing his hands.

'Hang on, I'll bring you a seat.'

Maweu unfolded the table chair and sat down. Mathembo had said nothing about Nzivele, an indication that she wanted to avoid confronting him with a hot issue. She behaved as if everything was fine. He was sure, he saw it in her face and heard it in her voice, she was happy to see him. His eyes avoided hers, but occasionally they met and he noticed in hers that motherly love she always had for him. He felt more at home. But he dared not ask where Nzivele was.

'I'll inform Nzivele's father,' she said, and walked away, behind the barn. Maweu swallowed. Now the right answer came: he would ask his wife to return home, then they would talk about Simon Mosi. They would also discuss her letter.

The short figure of Mbalu burst into the compound from a different direction, stirring up Maweu's nerves. Maweu came up on his feet and waited for Mbalu's greeting. Mbalu carried a large piece of cassava in his hand. He came over and shook hands with Maweu, looking quite happy to see him, too. The handshake was firm. Maweu hadn't thought that these parents of Nzivele's would receive him warmly like this, as if nothing had gone wrong. He saw the features of his wife on Mbalu's face. The mother returned from the same direction she had gone, and Mbalu asked her to give him a knife with which to peel the cassava. He wanted to eat a bit of it, raw.

Age sets in quickly, Maweu thought, noting that the old man had grown more grey hair recently. But he looked strong and jolly – the mother too. Both were happy-looking, good folk, close to each other as if they had married only the other month. Maweu wondered whether these two ever quarrelled between themselves. He felt ashamed that he and his Nzivele could not reach the harmony these old people had. Why? What was the formula for living happily with each other?

The contented face of Mbalu looked at the milk-white body of the cassava he had peeled. Mbalu split the cassava in the middle, twice, coming up with four slices. Getting to his feet, he brought the cassava to Maweu. 'It's a nice cassava,' he challenged, 'take a bit of it, please.'

Maweu cleared his throat and broke off one slice, his handsome face brightening. Mbalu took another piece to his wife, then returned to his seat. The three sat under the shade of the large tree. Mathembo sat on the ground, facing away from her son-in-law. Mbalu broke a piece of the cassava with his teeth and started chewing it soundly enough for Maweu to hear. Maweu took a bite of his and drowned his sense of hearing with his own chewing. He caught the sight of Mathembo's cheeks working vigorously on her portion of the cassava. There was long silence in which the three chewed the cassava patiently as though it was an act of allegiance that they must eat together first before they started tackling the Nzivele matter. Yet, no one had, so far, said anything about her. It was after half-past two in the afternoon. Following the greeting and the cassava allegiance, Mbalu had excused himself. 'While your mother finds something for food, I'd like to finish the piece of work I was doing,' he told Maweu and rose to his feet. They had asked Maweu about his mother and relatives. While Maweu told them about the family, they nodded, asking more questions. Maweu was sure that after the family questions, then they would come up with something about Nzivele. But no, it wasn't their wish, yet.

It had taken Nzivele's mother time to prepare a good lunch. In the meantime, Maweu had taken a short walk to the Kangundo shops, hoping that he would run into his wife, or meet someone who could tell him something about her. But he met nobody. Hardly anyone knew him here, anyway. He returned home and found the lunch nearly ready. Shortly afterwards, Mbalu came from the garden, looking rather tired. The three sat at the table and after Mbalu had said the grace, they set upon their lunch. They had their *nzenga*, polished and lightly ground maize that looked like rice, which they ate with sour milk.

While they ate, Mbalu kept them busy with stories about his youth, and how difficult life was in those days. It was clear to Maweu that these two had taken it that he had come with an intention of spending the night with them. But that was not Maweu's plan. He wanted to return home the same day, if it was possible.

'Where's your wife?' Mbalu finally broke into the heart of the matter. Mathembo had already cleared the table and was back, sitting with them. The room had good light from two windows on either side. It was a small, ten-by-twelve foot, neatly kept room. On the walls hung a number of framed pictures of Mbalu and his family, and another one in which he was in military uniform. He had fought in the Second World War.

Maweu echoed the same question to himself, 'Where's your wife?' He cleared his throat, adjusted his tie, fidgeted in his seat, seeking bravery to face the situation. He caught Mbalu's eyes fast on him.

'I thought she had come here.' Maweu sat up.

'Did you find her here?' asked Mbalu.

'No. Where did she go? She wrote to me, saying that she had come to live with you.'

'Why did she leave her home?' It seemed that it was Mbalu who was going to ask all the questions. His wife sat at a distance from them, making a basket, but listening keenly.

'I thought she told you.' Maweu braced himself.

'She didn't.'

'She should have told you.' He had his full courage back. 'We quarrelled over an issue and she ran away.'

'What was the fight about?'

After all, Maweu thought, she must have told them about the fight. He thought over his words, looking for a way round the problem of how to introduce the cause of the fight.

'We fought over her behaviour,' he said finally.

'What behaviour?'

Maweu made a big sigh. Mathembo halted making the basket in order to hear everything well.

'Did she tell you about somebody called Simon Mosi?'

'Who?' Mathembo asked loudly, turning to face Maweu, with pain in her face.

'Simon Mosi.'

'No,' they answered in unison.

'Oh, I see . . . '

'What about him?' Mbalu asked, disturbed.

'First, I didn't want to believe it,' Maweu continued after some silence. 'But I had to believe it later when things became too obvious.' He looked in their faces. They looked like people who had chewed quinine.

Maweu went on now, straight. 'Nzivele has been seen many times with that man – that Simon Mosi. In the end, it was no more a secret. I asked her about it, but she denied it . . . Then we quarrelled and I slapped her. Her relationship with my mother, too, has been terrible . . . '

Maweu returned in the evening, without seeing Nzivele. There had been a struggle between Mbalu and his wife when Mbalu said that his daughter had left home the previous day for Machakos and had not returned home. Mathembo didn't like the manner in which her husband had put it, implying that their daughter was running wild. She would have liked him to say that Nzivele had probably gone to see a relative or something . . . the kind of lie that protects a good name . . . But, Mbalu was a straightforward man . . . The details of his daughter's conduct had infuriated him. Maweu had tried to tell them everything, beginning with the dances, the collapse of their home plans, Nzivele's failure to pay the workers, her bitter disagreements with his mother and her negligence about taking care of the old woman.

Maweu was very uneasy about Nzivele's absence from home. He suspected that she had gone to meet Mosi because it appeared that Simon Mosi had been missing from his home for three days as well . . . Maweu had been told that Mosi had gone to Nairobi to see a sick relative.

'They must be together,' Maweu said and ground his teeth together, listening to the growing bitterness inside him. At one time, sitting in the bus returning to Machakos, he had felt like jumping out through the window and . . . or doing some damage of some kind. All right, Mbalu had listened and tried to sympathise with him, but that didn't help anything. The answer was still in Nzivele's hands. Now he felt, even if she had decided to leave him for ever, they should, at least, meet and say goodbye . . . It was not right to cut off everything like that. At least, she should also come home and collect her clothes, then quit, not to keep him in some kind of suspense.

'As parents,' Shadrak Mbalu had told him, 'there is very little we can do to change Nzivele's conduct, apart from talking to her and making her try to see the mistake. She is a grown-up person who has now learnt to ignore our advice if she doesn't like it and take her own course. Nzivele's mother and I here would like to do everything we could to give happiness to your marriage but we have our own limitations. No one likes to hear that his child is a thief . . . '

Both parents had advised Maweu to go home and return the next weekend. By then, they hoped, Nzivele would have come back and they would have talked to her. He had seen the helplessness in their faces regarding what they could do to change Nzivele's behaviour. 'She is your burden,' the words of Pastor Joana Mawia haunted him.

At Machakos, Silvesta Maweu checked everywhere he thought Nzivele might be. No, she wasn't any where. He walked, still looking for her, until he was too tired, until it was dark, then he had another problem – accommodation, because he couldn't get transport to Koola at that time. Finally, he ended up in a lodging. Somehow, he was afraid of going home without Nzivele. His mother was also waiting for her.

Voices in the lodging filled his mind, cursing him and demanding, 'Maweu, where is your wife? Why did you do that?' But the words of his friend, Wambua, also followed him, 'Silvesta, you must learn to forgive yourself; for, nobody else can do that. You are the only one who can understand and forgive yourself, then begin it anew.'

'But what else could I have done?' He tried to console himself.

The following morning, he woke up early and started walking again, looking for Nzivele. Every time, he thought, she must be arriving here, or catching transport there, or walking along that street. But Swastika Nzivele was nowhere at Machakos.

CHAPTER
12

◆ ◆ ◆ ◆

It was now three weeks since Silvesta Maweu had returned to Mombasa. He had not yet succeeded in finding Nzivele, and had started losing hope that she would ever come back. But things were becoming difficult for him . . . and he had left home extremely worried about the condition of his mother's health. Kalunde had started complaining of the same pains that she had before. He thought she looked like someone about to go . . .

Something else bad had struck Kalunde's home. One night, while she was sleeping, someone, or some people had knocked off her door with a large stone and poured into the house with a torch in their hands. The next thing Kalunde had heard, between her screams, was the sound of the chickens being rounded up. However much she cried, the burglars took no notice. They went about their business with confidence. Kalunde decided to risk her life. She had slipped down from her bed and gone out of the room to the living room to face whoever had come.

'Let them kill me,' she thought.

But as Soon as she had popped her head into the room, a bright torch light burst into her face, blinding her completely, then something heavy had hit her in the face, driving her back. She had fallen against the wall and dropped to the floor. A hard voice had rung in her ears. 'If you want to die, come up again.'

'Why don't you just finish me off, in God's name?' Kalunde had cried from the floor. But nobody had answered her. She had screamed at the top of her voice, but who could hear her screams? The nearest neighbour was half a mile away; and the woman whom Maweu had left behind to take care of Kalunde was not around. She hadn't shown up for the previous three days. There was some kind of struggle as the thieves ran out of the house. Someone must have stumbled and fallen hard by the door. The next thing that Kalunde had heard was the clucking of the chickens outside the house, then footsteps had started running away, followed by still silence . . .

There had been twelve chickens which Maweu had brought over a month before and left in the custody of Kiki, the house maid. Maweu had planned to start keeping chickens again as the business had proved lucrative within the short time that Nzivele had tried it. At the end of the year he had planned to have, at least, a hundred and fifty chickens.

The theft hadn't ended there. A week later, the thieves had returned, this time to the garden, stealing all the *kathuku* bananas that were about ready for harvesting. They had dug up the cassavas, uprooting everything in search of anything edible. In the end, there was absolutely nothing left behind for Kalunde. There was a suspicion that Kiki must have been behind that theft in one way or another. She had given up work, claiming that she feared being attacked in the night.

This was a mean year, a year of great famine. The whole country, north and south, east and west, had fallen into great drought, a drought that could be seen everywhere, in everything you looked at. Gardens were stripped of anything edible, from leaves to roots. And a *muthyuuko* disease came with the famine. It was a disease that, when it attacked a cow, proved fatal within a week. On the fifth day, the animal would begin to spin around, the whole day long, then drop dead within the next two or three days.

A drop of water became invaluable. People stopped taking baths. You met them and, when they passed you, a thick, very stunning smell followed them. The old became older faster. Death toll rose, old people dropped dead on every side, children too. Miscarriages plagued the countryside. Poor mothers, and those who had no relatives working in towns, began to disappear, killed by one disease or another. Quarrels, fights and divorces swept through every village. Churches were full. Schoolgirls sought marriage or eloped . . .

'Famine,' Kalunde had often said, 'is revolutionary.' But Joana Mawia had also added, 'Want alters morals.'

Cyclones arrived, beating through the country, starting gently at ten in the morning and maturing in the afternoon. They came, spinning, whistling, building giant upright pipes of red dust and straws. They constantly swept clouds of dust over Koola shops, threatening to uproot the roofs and hurl them miles away. They entered houses and started fires that burnt down people's homes. When they swept over you, they punished you with sand, forcing it and dust into your ears, eyes, and nose, while you held yourself against a tree.

Storms of hunger . . . It was Kalunde herself who knew the pains of famine. This was not the only famine she had seen. In fact, this particular famine was not the horror that people thought it was . . . Kalunde had seen worse, because she was a living history of one famine disaster. But why had another famine returned to her life, especially at its close, as if to make a second bracket with that other famine that had struck during her childhood?

'Misfortune,' she said aloud, sitting in her lonely house one evening, 'misfortune seems to love perching in certain homes. Mine, for example . . . Where's the end of this path?' It must have been after midnight, for she had sat by the fireplace until the wood had burned down completely, and the embers were reduced into ashes. She thought more and more about her present misfortune. Today, she was very hungry. Her hunger reminded her, particularly this night, of the famine that had taken her mother away. Hunger had caused the death of her mother, Mathei, just as Kalunde remembered the water that had brought about the great loss of her own family. It all returned to her mind, as vividly as when it had happened. At that moment, it didn't seem to have happened so long ago . . . she could see it still . . .

Many years back, when Kalunde was a small girl, about ten years old, a catastrophic famine had struck throughout the country, hitting each home mercilessly and scattering the people either through death or by driving them out and away in every direction in search of food, in a struggle for survival. Some people walked until they fell down and starved to death, or were killed and eaten by wild animals. Mothers walked, carrying their children until the children starved to death on their mother's backs. Some mothers were forced to abandon a child here or there, just to make the burden bearable. For, there comes a time in one's life, when the heavens pour down disaster, that one has just to take things as they come, grave as they may be.

Mathei, Kalunde's mother, had found herself in that misfortune. Her husband had fallen sick and died of one of the many plagues that accompanied such famines. In the record of the Akamba people, there were many famines of that kind. For example, the famine of Kakuti, the famine of Yua Ya Ndata, the famine of Nzalukye, and so on. Mathei lived in the famine of Kakuti.

One morning, Mathei was forced to take her two children, Kalunde and Muthama and go, just anywhere looking for anyone, any man with food who could adopt her and her children. She had walked for many days, trying to economise on the little food that they had carried, until that, too, got finished. Then they had to begin begging, also trying to eat anything they could lay their hands on – roots, tree-bark or certain leaves. This was not sufficient to sustain their lives. Mathei fell sick and the burden of her son, Muthama, became overbearing. However, one day, Mathei came to a village that, apparently, had food. She went and begged for something to eat. An elderly man distinguished himself from the villagers and took the wretched family to his house and asked his wife to give Mathei food and shelter for a day or two.

'We are looking for a man to adopt us,' Kalunde remembered having heard from Mathei's mouth, saying the words to that man. 'We have no family and food where we come from.'

The man listened to Mathei patiently and sympathetically. He looked at the children, then at Mathei, and walked out of the house without saying a word. His wife wasn't in the house at that time. The man didn't come back for a number of hours; however, eventually he returned. But he didn't give his answer until the next day in the morning hours.

'I'll take you,' he replied.

But one thing was obvious: the man's wife, Wathi, didn't like it. Wathi had three children, Muthungu, the eldest son, who was about fifteen years old, and two daughters. Wathi would then have had nine children altogether, if smallpox hadn't claimed the lives of the other children.

For nearly two weeks, Wathi did nothing about it, in spite of Mathei's determination to help in any labour she had been given. The family kept a large farm in which they grew every kind of food they needed. They were lucky to occupy a piece of land, by the bottom of the Matiliku hill, that had a valley with water throughout the year, even in the most dry years. In this valley, Wathi's husband, Mwambambi, had a large sugarcane plantation, where he also grew sweet potatoes, arrowroot, cassava, and so on. He had a good herd of livestock, too.

One morning, Wathi and Mathei went to work in the garden together. Muthungu accompanied his mother to bring home some sugarcane for the family before taking the livestock out for grazing. He had liked Mathei since she arrived. But he had already sensed his mother's dislike for her. This morning, the two women had walked together silently from the house, for about two miles, accompanied by Muthungu who had already become suspicious that these two might pick a fight when they were left on their own.

Muthungu had been right. Something terrible was bound to happen eventually. After Wathi and Mathei had given Muthungu the sugarcane he needed to take home, he made as if he had gone away. But he turned at another point in the forest and came back to hide in the sugarcane plantation nearby. He had a long time to wait. Every time he decided to go away, his nerves told him to stay.

Mathei was busy digging sweet potatoes unaware that Wathi was planning to attack her. Wathi had fetched a heavy stone and was studying Mathei's movements. She worked behind Mathei, waiting for the right opportunity. So, this time when Mathei sank to the ground after stretching her back, Wathi grabbed the stone and approached Mathei from behind. Had Muthungu been fully attentive, his mother would not have succeeded in her wicked deed. But he heard the sound of the blow. Wathi had struck Mathei at the back of the neck, fatally. Mathei hardly made any sound. Meanwhile, Wathi ran out of sight, then started screaming that someone had killed Mathei and ran into the sugarcane plantation. She was not aware that her son had heard everything.

'Mathei!' Muthungu screamed, running to see what had happened to her; but Mathei was already dead. Realising that her son must know all about the incident, Wathi plunged herself into the sugarcane plantation and went dead silent, hiding. Muthungu ran home as fast as he could to report the matter. The first person he found at home was the young Kalunde. He fell down out of breath and cried before Kalunde, telling her that her mother had been killed by his own mother.

Muthungu and his mother never reconciled. Three years after the incident, Muthungu ran away with Kalunde to Kyandumbi to live with Kalunde's aunt, after the famine was over. Kalunde's brother, Muthama, didn't survive for more than a year after his mother's death. In those days, too, child mortality was very high.

Years after, Kalunde and Muthungu had gotten married. Kalunde passed her fingers over her eyes after remembering how her mother had died '. . . Whatever God's mind is . . .,' she thought.

Had it not been for the modern means of food distribution and earning money for one's living, this famine, like the Kakuti, would have swept away many more lives. But times had changed. Those families with people working in the cities brought food to the countryside. At least, even though the poor ones died of malnutrition, those in good hands, like Wathi, survived. Had it not been for Silvesta Maweu, Kalunde would have gone with the others. That did not mean, however, that she was entirely 'in good hands'. Where would she have been, she thought, if it were not for the pastor's help?

Still Kalunde thought in the womb of the silent night, 'Why has misfortune followed me like this? Where is the end of this path?' She sought for the answer under the light of her thoughts, but it was dark, everything was pitch dark . . .

Since Kiki had stopped working, Kalunde had made no effort to write to Maweu about it. She thought it would be wiser not to disturb him, as he had been home so often in the last months and he had expressed his fear that if he continued absenting himself from work like that, and always presenting his employer with his problems, he might lose the job. That was the last thing Kalunde could wish to happen to her son. So, she sat over the matter, feeling that, after all, she could manage things on her own for a time, especially with the constant help of the Mawias who, from time to time, sent her food.

One afternoon when Kalunde had been waiting in vain for the pastor's wife to come to draw water for her, she decided to go down to the river to draw the water for herself. She had had nothing to eat or drink since the previous day. She picked up a small gourd and walked down slowly, in spite of some bodily pains, till she came to the well. This was another period when the well had shrunk deep into the sand. She found nobody at the well. Only a few more weeks of drought, then this well would dry up too, then people would have to start walking miles and miles for a gourd of water.

Fearing the depth of the well, Kalunde lingered around waiting for a villager to come to help her. But it seemed nobody was ever going to come. In the end, she thought she might as well try for herself. If she filled up the gourd, she wouldn't be able to bring it up to the surface. So she decided to fill it half-way.

She never got to the bottom of the well. Somewhere she made a wrong move, slipped and fell. The heavy fall shook the walls of the well, a whole wall tore down and buried her.

CHAPTER

13

◆ ◆ ◆ ◆

Kalunde had died on a Wednesday, but her burial was not to be before Saturday. Silvesta Maweu arrived home on Thursday evening. It was Pastor Joana Mawia himself who had travelled to Mombasa to break the sad news to Maweu.

A large crowd came to Kalunde's burial, led by Pastor Joana Mawia. It had been decided that Kalunde should be buried under the mango tree where she had been so fond of resting. The red soil from the grave covered the mango stem half-way.

'Life has three seasons.' The pastor broke the silence of the hushed crowd. 'The season of birth. The season of growing up and doing the earthly things. Then comes the last season: the time of death.

'As our parents gathered once upon a time to celebrate the birth of our sister, Kalunde, that was the very first mark that our sister would one day leave us. That day is today. I have known Kalunde for many years. And in those years I have known her, Kalunde has lived a complete life, a good example of living love, as a woman who believed in the integrity of life. One who gave no material wealth to the people of this village; but one who has left a legacy of love behind, love that no amount of money can buy. She has gone, but Kalunde remains living in every one of us. She has gone nowhere far or strange, she has simply gone home where we are all bound for. For, it is at a time like this, that each one of us realises the bond between his life and that of the next world. And all of this world is not complete until the day such as today comes . . . This is the time, when we take back what we have inherited from this world, the time of going back, simply as we came, into that first land . . .'

Silvesta Maweu felt moved. He would not have wept at all, if the pastor had not spoken. He had lived these last years prepared for his mother's death one day. Kalunde was dead, lying on the bed she had merely slept on for years. But the words of the pastor hit Maweu deeply somewhere deep inside, chasing tears out easily, naturally. He didn't want to make any sound while crying; but the automation of all the grief shook and drove a sound out of his inside. He sobbed aloud; the sound of a son crying for his dead mother, trying to express the bond between a child and his mother . . .

But, in that very moment, farther back from the crowd, erupted another louder crying sound of another broken heart. A woman burst into tears and fell on the ground. She was one of the late arrivals who had come and stood far off, listening. The crying woman was Swastika Nzivele!

At first, there was a big hush, then a murmuring followed the discovery of who the woman was. Nzivele cried out bitterly as if she had run into the dead body of her own mother. Nobody had seen her arrival; and nobody would have expected her to come, not even Silvesta Maweu, for, ever since the night of their fight, he had not seen her.

At this juncture the pastor, too, lost his heart and wept, particularly when he saw and heard Nzivele. A number of elders took Maweu, Nzivele and the pastor to Maweu's house and closed the door behind them.

Nzivele went up to Maweu and the couple cried together, wrapped in each other's arms. But there was another man with his hand on them - Pastor Joana Mawia, feeling a profound love for these two; in that moment he felt for these two as if they were his own children.

He let them cry, watching them, as his own tears fell with theirs. Swastika Nzivele and Silvesta Maweu stood closely against each other, their hands joined together as the pastor said the last prayer. It was after they had lowered Kalunde's body into her grave.

'Our loving God,' the pastor spoke loudly, in a deep masculine voice, 'we have escorted our sister back to you because your time has come for her to return home. Our sister has undergone many earthly tribulations of which all of us here are witnesses. In man's judgement, we acclaim her as a great soul that came here to benefit many people. Please, take her, and for the sake of your children, for Lord you are the love and the footstep that Kalunde tried to follow, keep her together with the good ones. Give her what she didn't get from this world. Through her hand, you have proved that love is supreme.

'Kalunde was like a well in a dry village, where all came to draw spiritual renewal that earthly riches cannot give man. For, all riches of the world are nothing, unless they be crowned with love for people. Such love as we pray that you give us to continue to see hope where there is despair; renewal where there is exhaustion.

'Let the spirit that lived in our sister live in a thousand others, that in the end, they should leave hope for humanity. We will cover her earthly body with the earthly blanket with which you clothed the beautiful soul . . .

'It is your love that has called Maweu's wife from wherever she had been. At this moment, we pray that Kalunde's spirit should live in them and that they should find everlasting comfort with each other. Give them children, Lord, we beseech you, you who shall never let anyone who comes to you down . . .

'In the name of the one God, through his son, Jesus

Christ, we ask this . . . '

The crowd put the *Amen* seal to the prayer.

Exactly twelve months after Kalunde's burial, Swastika Nzivele bore a daughter to Silvesta Maweu, and they named the daughter Kalunde. The name of Simon Mosi had disappeared from Maweu's marriage as though Kalunde had taken it away with her to the grave.

The coffee, and the chickens, and the home that Maweu and his wife had always wanted, all began to spring from the ground as though the death of Kalunde had become great manure and water for their struggle. Nzivele never followed her husband to live in Mombasa in the five years that he continued to work until he gave up the job to come to develop his farm and live permanently in the country. He constructed a big dam nearby, big enough for every single form of irrigation he needed in his farm.

Pastor Joana Mawia grew closer to them. Nzivele had two more children, sons, before God closed her womb.

Printed in the United States
By Bookmasters